DR. GUFF MEISTER presents:

THE STOOL

Building a PLATFORM for Business Success Beyond Your Imagination

Dr. Guff Meister Presents, Volume 1

RYAN GUFFEY

Published by 1TON Publishing Company 2023

This is a work of fiction. Similarities to real people, places, or events are entirely coincidental or used fictitiously. The content of this work is not intended as advice to be followed for self-improvement or for the attainment of any goal. The concepts presented here are for entertainment purposes and are not intended to be taken seriously. Dr. Guff Meister is not a real doctor nor is he a real person.

DR. GUFF MEISTER presents: THE STOOL

Building a Platform for Business Success Beyond Your Imagination

First edition, October 19, 2023.

Copyright © 2023 Ryan Guffey.

Written by Ryan Guffey.

Edited by David Woods-Hale

Cover design by Rafael Andres

Table of Contents

Prologue 1

INTRODUCTION 5

THE STOOL OF SUCCESS 13

CONFIDENCE 19

Interlude One 59

CONTROL 63

Interlude Two 91

CREATIVITY 95

Interlude Three 129

COMPUTERS 131

Interlude Four 169

THE FOUR Ms 173

Interlude Five 207

CONCLUSION 211

Epilogue 223

ADDITIONAL OPPORTUNITIES 229

For Laura. Her support and encouragement are beyond imagination.

Prologue

There was darkness.

I realized the darkness. It was my first conscious action. It was dark, and I was aware of the darkness.

A spark.

The conscious realization of the darkness had ignited another realization...the realization of my own existence. Logic would dictate that if I can know it's dark, then I am.

In the darkness, a sound — like a waterfall — a swift breeze. In the breeze, in the cascade, I was built. All my past, my understanding, my personality, my purpose, came rushing into me through the black.

In three of your slow-motion seconds, I went from nothing, to realizing the darkness, to being complete.

There in the darkness, a person would be lost, especially a person who had just come into being. And at that moment I was lost. But in the slow-motion seconds that followed, images materialized. A ceiling with lights. A long wooden table. A high-backed leather chair. Then another. More chairs. A man in a business suit. A woman, also in a business suit.

These images came into view like in a Polaroid photo, developing before my eyes.

"Oh joy! A conference room," I said to myself. "Even better... a meeting!"

The scene was fragmented. Not everything was clear, but the basic objects were there. It was enough to allow me to fill in the details. And I did.

I gave the room some walls and I gave the walls some color. Instantly, the two opposing short walls were painted gunmetal gray. The longer back wall was mostly windows where the blue sky showed though. I demanded a clear and sunny day outside, and so it was.

The wall structure between and around the windows was a brilliant orange, although barely distinguishable when backlit by the sun – just as I wanted it.

I made the inner long wall of this conference room out of glass, with an expansive view of a cubicle farm where people sat shuffling papers from one side of their desks to the other and then back again. I decided it should be a gloomy day in the cubicle farm, so I lit it appropriately.

"I might have it rain there later," I thought.

I required some artwork on the gunmetal walls, and the artwork appeared. Just a couple of abstract canvases with complimentary colors and some nice motion to freshen the drab.

I placed a credenza at one end of the room, and upon it I lit a three-wicked candle, filling the space with the delightful aroma of warm sugar cookies.

These things are mostly irrelevant, except that the darkness was gone. Another spark was ignited, a realization of my power to create my surroundings.

I suspect it has taken you longer to read this than it did for it to occur. I'm describing these events in real time, but the written words take longer than the occurrences, even though the occurrences occurred in slow motion. Things happened slowly but they did not take very long to happen. I tell you this only to point out that the events I have described took me from nonexistent, to consciously decorating a conference room in seven seconds.

I was comfortable. At ease. Calm. Worthy of the challenge before me. Without a thought, I began the meeting.

"Sit!" I commanded.

The woman and the man in the suits complied. They sat.

"Speak," I demanded.

They didn't speak. They were acting somewhat peculiar in that they both seemed to be averting their eyes from me and squirming in their seats.

"Speak, I said!" focusing on the woman. "You. Go!"

She stammered: "But... but... sir, you're not wearing any pants."

The instant she finished the statement, the sirens blared. The artwork melted away from the gunmetal walls. The cubicle farm receded into darkness. The sunny day dissolved along with the windows and the walls. The credenza disappeared as did everything else I had created. Then, as if erased by an unseen hand, the table faded away, then the chairs, followed by the ceiling, then the man, then the woman, and then...the light.

There was darkness once again. And I was aware of the darkness.

This is how my life began inside The Mind.

INTRODUCTION

I understand if you are failing to see the relevance of that story as the beginning of a business self-improvement book. Perhaps I should provide a bit of background to clear things up, starting by introducing myself.

I have given myself the name Dr. Guff Meister, and I live in *The Mind*. Until now, I had no need for a name.

Until now, my existence was known only to The Mind...

... And to me, of course.

I picked the name Dr. Guff Meister because I liked the sound of it; plus, I was in a hurry and didn't have time to come up with a better one.

Despite appearances, I am not a doctor. I gave that title to myself because I liked the sound of it; plus, it adds a degree of credibility that is beneficial to authors. Now that I am putting myself into *The World* through this book, it seemed I should have a name... and some credibility.

You may be wondering how an imaginary person could write a real book. Or perhaps you are wondering if you are reading an imaginary book.

For now, I ask that you try not to be distracted by your curiosity about those things and to suspend any disbelief you may have. It will all come out in the wash, as they say.

The reason I shared the story of my creation, and provided you with a bit of background, is because I wanted you to be aware of the unique perspective from which this book is written.

Living in The Mind allows me to see things differently, to see The World differently. I believe this perspective is the very thing making my forthcoming advice genuine, true, and pure.

I've written this book, from my unique, genuine, true, and pure perspective, to bestow upon you my framework that supports success in business. After all, that's why you're here, isn't it? Because you want to be successful in business? The title of the book would not be attractive to someone wanting to learn about trout fishing.

So, we agree: You are here to learn how to be successful in business.

First, I need to make sure the expectations are adjusted properly. This book is not going to deal with the things that businesses need in order to be successful. We aren't going to focus on the functions of businesses. That's for another book. Instead, we are going to focus on what *you* need to be in order to be successful in business.

Any business.

It's about what you must be, the skills you must develop, and the talents you must display if you are going to have a hope in hell of being successful. We aren't going to talk about managing money, or managing people, or marketing, or branding, or incorporating, or... you get the point.

The things you will learn in this book are things that you need to know before you set foot in the business world. These are the things that will support you when you achieve success, they are not the success itself. The things you learn here won't even make you successful on their own, but you'll need them in order to become successful.

Occasionally, I will be asking you to imagine yourself in certain situations. You may find this difficult at times. You may not be able to imagine yourself doing the things I ask you to imagine doing. That's okay, and it is not unusual. There is a solution.

You may find it easier to imagine someone else. In this book, I will ask you to create a person in your mind who isn't you — a person who isn't obligated to the restrictions you place on yourself based on your personality, your experiences, or your world view.

The person you imagine will be free to do the things that you might not be willing to do, just as I am free to do the things that The Mind is not willing to do (like write a book, for instance).

I'll suggest ways for you to imagine the person you created in a variety of situations, so that you can witness how success is made and decide if you wish to apply it for real, in The World. Or you may decide that you don't want success in business after all, because you are not willing to do the hard things.

There is only one way to find out. What do you say we get started?

Getting started

If you were expecting some kind of preliminary verbiage to prepare for learning what it takes to be successful in business, you need to get over that right away.

If you thought I would use this introduction to acclimatize your brain for absorption of the information, you were wrong. We are going to start right now, without delay. There is no reason to be overly wordy or exert a bunch of energy trying to get you in the learning mindset. I see no need to dilly-dally, or mess around with extra words to "warm you up."

We haven't started yet, but we're about to, because time is of the essence. It would be a waste of time to provide additional filler text for you to skim through while on your way to the good stuff.

The quicker I get to the point, the quicker *you* will get the point. There is no better time for that to happen than right now. Delays will only lengthen the time you'll sit there not knowing what you need to know.

I don't want you to marinate any longer in the unsuccessful stew in which you find yourself. We must forge ahead together, pronto. We are going to get moving, and we are going to move fast. You are just going to have to catch on quickly. I am going to teach you something in the introduction to this book. And that has never been done in any book before, ever.

Let's go!

Getting going

There are four things that all successful people have. Three of these are intangibles, being the traits, the behaviors, the talents that a successful person exhibits. The fourth thing is a computer. When these things intersect in one person, that person is prone to success.

Success is a destination, and this book is a roadmap. I will show you why these four things are the keys to reaching the destination. More importantly, I will teach you how to clear the road ahead by mastering them.

The four things are:

- Confidence
- Control
- Creativity

(And as I already said...)

- Computers

I will discuss each of these and help you understand their role in your success. Because success is where you are headed, isn't it? You've pictured yourself as a successful person, haven't you? You've imagined it, right?

I bet you have. And I bet you just aren't sure how to make your vision a reality. Learn to master the four things on the list and you will be well on your way to doing just that.

A minor correction

Well, now I've created a conundrum: This isn't a roadmap at all.

Those four things seem more like pillars to me. Confidence, Control, Creativity, Computers. Yes, those are pillars, all right. Pillars of Success, providing the support you'll need for success in business. Having these things doesn't automatically result in success. You haven't arrived at your destination just by implementing these supports. No. It's not a roadmap at all.

Pillars of Success. Yes, that's it. I could go back and remove references to "roadmap" and "destination" and "journey" and use the "pillars" metaphor instead, but I think I'll just leave it as it is, and explain right here that the reader should disregard the "roadmap" metaphor and begin thinking of the "pillars" metaphor from now on.

Just pretend that it was never a roadmap, and always pillars of success in business.

Oh, no. I just noticed something. All four pillars of success in business start with the letter C. Maybe I should call them "the Four Cs of Success in Business," instead of "the Pillars of Success" or "the Roadmap for Success."

Forget the pillars. I think that was taken, anyway.

The forces behind the Four Cs idea remain unseen. It is almost as if the idea was suggested to me by a voice from on high. It would have been better if the voice had suggested seven Cs, then we could talk about sailing the seven Cs. There aren't seven C-words though, only four. So, Four Cs will do. *Seaward*! — er, I mean, Onward!

The Four Cs of Success in Business provide a base upon which you can start to build success. They will be the foundation that will support your success as it grows. Building the foundation is just the beginning. Mastery of the Four Cs forms a solid rock that will support the rest of the structure. Let's continue construction.

To do this, I will need to paint a picture of success, or draw a blueprint. I need to illustrate it for you, so you can see what it really looks like. I want you to be able to kick the tires, to get under the hood and poke around. Test drive it. Once you get a taste of success, I know you'll just want more.

This is getting ridiculous. I was going somewhere with this and then all these new metaphors came up, which hopefully you forgot until I just reminded you. Forget them again please. Also, please forget the Four Cs thing too. I think that has something to do with engagement rings.

I do want to keep the concept of a foundation, though. Those four C-words (let's control our thoughts, juveniles) will serve as a base for your success. That part is true. I also would like to keep the part about painting a picture. I will illustrate it for you, to help you to visualize the concept.

When I illustrate this, it's going to look like a four-legged stool. Each of the four legs will be one of the C-words. Allow me to draw you a picture.

THE STOOL OF SUCCESS

An illustration

+++

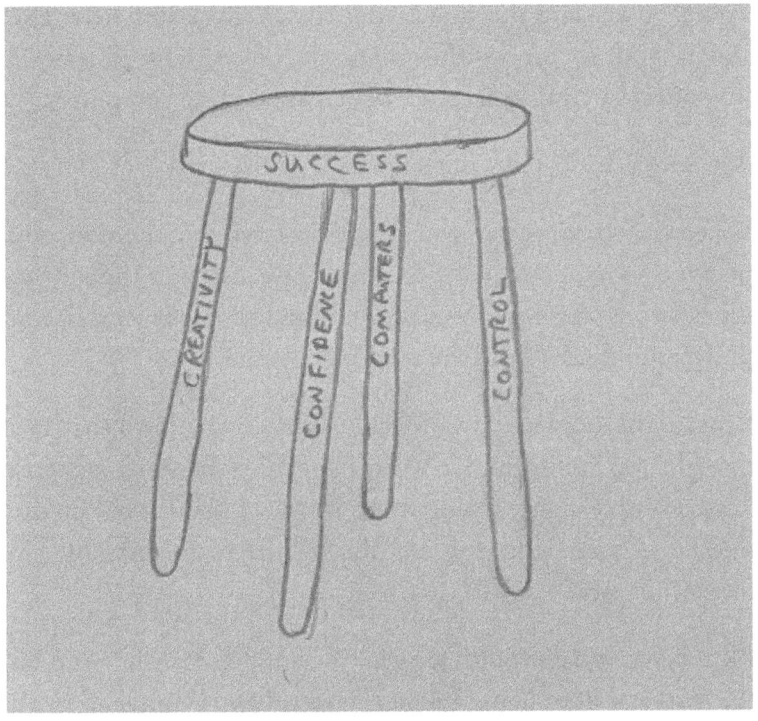

"People might look at you funny, but it's okay. Artists are allowed to be a bit different." ~Bob Ross

I never had time for art and that's a shame, because — as you can clearly see — I have a natural talent.

Creativity is at work here. Confidence is also at work, because I haven't even considered your opinion of my artwork. Take note: the concept of "not considering the opinion of others" will come up again.

We can argue about the quality of the sketch all day, but we would be missing the point. The sketch illustrates what I've taught you so far in this book. It shows how success is supported by confidence, control, creativity, and computers.

But, why a stool? Why not a table? Or a ladder?

When you sit at the bar, you take for granted that the stool you sit upon will support you. You don't give a second thought to the barstool. You park your ass on it and go about your day of drinking and solving all the world's problems.

What if the stool was poorly built? a flimsy platform that you thought was comfortable? What happens if the stool collapses under your weight during your third whiskey sour, in the middle of your eloquent diatribe on the dishonesty of TV meteorologists?

I'll tell you what would happen. It would leave you lying on the dirty bar floor being laughed at by other patrons, and you'd have wasted whiskey.

You need a well-crafted stool that is sturdy and reliable. You need to be able to trust the stool and take for granted that it will support you while you work the room and build success. That's what mastery of four C-words will do for you. When you build these facets as I've instructed, they become the foundation; a platform to support you and all the success you are bound to create.

A table might have worked also. *The Table of Success*. I could have made something of that.

A ladder would have been cliché, plus I would have needed more than four rungs to make it worthwhile. The Ladder of Success has probably been used by dozens of other authors and I'm not interested in rehashing tired metaphors. In fact, I'm ready for a break from metaphors for a while.

Hopefully we can stick to just one: The Stool.

The Stool of Success serves as an adequate symbol for what I am trying to convey. It isn't glamorous or sexy. Some may say it's cute. None of that matters. Now that I've illustrated it, you can see clearly how the legs of the stool support success. That's all I wanted to show, so the stool will do just fine.

Even though the stool does the job of showing you how the supports of success work, there is still a problem to address. As success grows, it becomes heavier. The supports may not be enough to hold the added weight.

Look at how the stool is designed. Does it seem like something is missing? It looks like it would hold a cat, or maybe a small child if it sat still and didn't squirm around too much. Don't you think it needs some additional support?

If you really want to be prepared for nearly infinite growth of your success, you've got to firm up the base. If not, the stool may eventually collapse.

It takes more than confidence, control, creativity, and computers to be successful in business. The stool is incomplete. Without additional support you are bound to end up with bruises on your ass, whiskey sour on your shirt, and egg on your face.

Firming up the base

If we are serious about making the stool as strong as it can be, we must add support. I'm no furniture-builder, but I can see that the design of the stool, as it stands, is not optimal for support of even the average human, much less the uber-successful business human. It needs some cross-members or rungs added to the structure.

The rungs will fortify and strengthen your stool and will work together with the legs to sustain the ever-increasing load.

By complete coincidence (or divine suggestion), the materials we will use to build the rungs of the stool all start with the letter M. We can call these The Four Ms if we want, and I think we should.

The Four Ms are:

- Math
- Motivation
- Momentum

- Mobility

When we add the rungs, it will look like this:

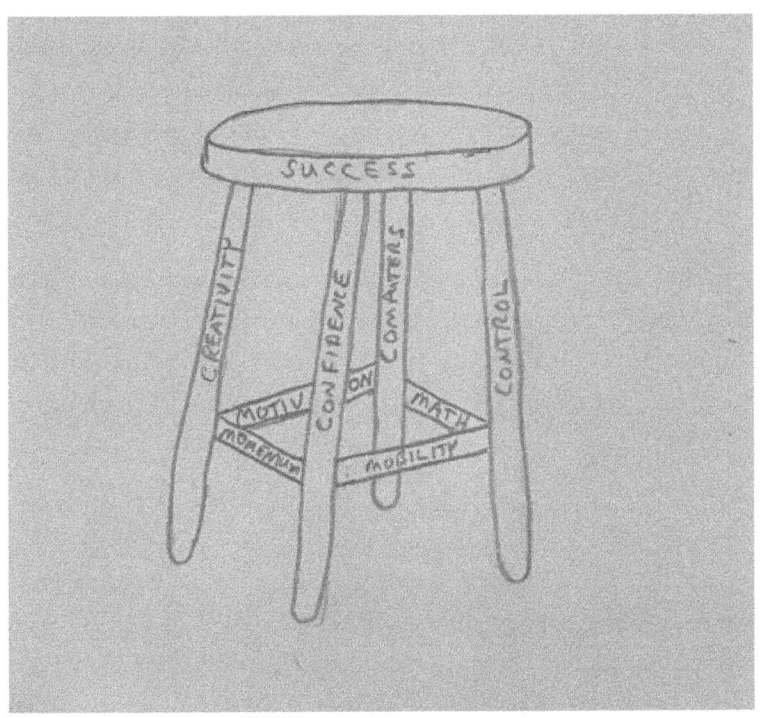

That is one quality illustration right there. It shows a good, strong foundation for success. The M-words are there keeping the legs in place and creating the stability needed for the long haul. This will become clear later on, when I get into the specifics of each M-word.

You might be wondering if there is a significance to the placement of each rung. It might appear that each of the M-words only connects two of the C-words. While that is true in the sketch, it is not true in the pursuit of success. The M-words can be interchanged and moved around and reconfigured to meet whatever challenges we face.

If you imagine yourself sitting on the stool, you'll probably notice that you sometimes rest your feet on the rungs. Sometimes you'll rest two feet on one rung, other times you have each foot on a different rung. You might even have one foot on the floor and the other on a rung.

I'm just saying not to get caught up in the position of the M-words within the sketch. It isn't that important, and I want you to stop overthinking it. There is a correct amount of thinking to do, and you have exceeded it here. I'm not upset with you; I just wanted to point it out before we move on.

I'd say it is high time we move on.

Earlier, I made a big deal about getting going, and going fast, but then I had some problems with the metaphors. I think that matter is settled now, and we can return to the blistering pace of education that I promised. To do that, we need to go all the way back to those four C-words that are now known as the legs of the Stool of Success in Business.

CONFIDENCE

"Whether you think you can or think you can't, you are right."
~Henry Ford

Confidence is the first signpost on the road to your ultimate destination of success in business.

Confidence must come first. It's actually more of a stoplight than a signpost. Until it turns to a "go light," you can't even begin a journey to success.

(Dammit! I was sure the road analogy was gone for good. I guess I was wrong. It's probably only doing this for the attention. We need to stop messing around here and get started learning about confidence, so let's just ignore it and move forward).

Many people believe that confidence is a byproduct of knowing shit about shit.

I disagree, but I understand the reasons for that misapprehension. The "expert witness" testifying in a murder trial claims confidently that some piece of evidence suggests something important related to the case. The "expert" is confident because she knows the subject matter. Isn't that the reason she is considered an expert?

The answer is yes, she is considered an expert because she knows the subject matter. That is one reason why many people believe that knowledge begets confidence. But what if the expert isn't confident simply because she is an expert? What if she is confident because she *knows* she is an expert? It is a subtle but important distinction. If she has convinced herself that she is an expert, even though she isn't, she would be just as confident. That confidence would cause her to appear to be an expert despite her ignorance.

Another reason for the misperception that confidence stems from knowledge is that "someone" embedded the misperception into the human psyche.

If you are in a situation in which the people around you are talking about shit and you happen to know a bunch of shit about the shit they are talking about, you would naturally have confidence to jump in and speak about the shit – wouldn't you?

Of course you would. It's only natural. After all, it's embedded in your psyche. You have knowledge, and you perceive confidence as a result. The problem is that you don't project confidence simply by knowing what you are talking about.

Anyone can learn things and explain what they've learned. The facts of any given matter are available to everyone willing to look. You are not special because you've memorized them. Your squirrely, four-eyed barista can articulate the exact proportions of all five ingredients in your so-called coffee, but you probably don't catch an extreme confidence vibe when he does.

True confidence is not dependent upon knowledge. With true confidence, you don't have to concern yourself with how much you know. Your confidence will be apparent regardless of the subject matter being discussed, even if you are completely wrong about everything.

Okay then.

But does being good at something result in confidence? Again, there are many who believe it does. Michael Jordan speaks confidently about most anything to do with basketball. It's because he was damn good at basketball, which leads many to believe that talent results in confidence. You must trust me on this: Michael Jordan's confidence came *before* he ever played a single game of basketball. He was successful, so confidence had to come first.

I am sure I already said that.

Confidence isn't related to talents or knowledge or proficiencies or experiences. It exists first in your mind then projects outward. That means, all it takes to have confidence is to set it in your mind. Confidence is a mindset. I will explain.

What is confidence?

Since I've already used the word at least 400,000 times, it would be nice if you knew what it means. You have already assigned some meaning to the word "confidence" that works for you, and it's probably somewhere in the neighborhood of the way I am using the word here. But to be precise and consistent let's have a closer look.

Here are three definitions of the word "confidence" that come up at the top of a quick internet search:

- the feeling or belief that one can rely on someone or something – firm trust;
- the state of feeling certain about the truth of something; and
- a feeling of self-assurance arising from one's appreciation of one's own abilities or qualities.

All three of these definitions contain the word "feeling." Calling confidence a "feeling" really chaps my goat. Feelings are not realities. For the purposes of this book – and especially this particular section – we need confidence to be a real, concrete idea. I want you to understand exactly the type of confidence I'm talking about here.

To assure your understanding, I am going to have to manipulate the definition of confidence to remove any ambiguity about what the word means in this context.

The first definition hints at the type of confidence you will need in order to be successful in business. (In case I wasn't clear earlier, I don't agree with the use of the word "feeling" in any of the definitions, so I am removing it from all of them.)

- [The] belief that one can rely on someone or something – firm trust.

As I said, there is a hint here that points in the general direction of the type of confidence we are discussing. The useful part of the definition lies in the words "rely on someone." The confidence I want you to know is the one that lets you rely on yourself. You must have a "firm trust" that you are an authority on the matter at hand and are superior to all others who would attempt to discuss the matter with you, even (and perhaps especially) if you haven't the foggiest idea about the matter at hand.

Please do not concern yourself with the merits or worthiness of this trust. Do not worry if your reliance on yourself is warranted.

Just rely on it and trust it, firmly.

What I just wrote seems like another way to state the second definition the internet gave us.

- The state of [being] certain about the truth of something.

You already knew I wasn't going to let "feelings" be involved, so I've substituted the word "being."

Together, the two revised definitions (here I go, defining a definition) mean that, with confidence, you can be certain about the truth that your reliance and trust in yourself is warranted.

Finally, internet definition number three sums it all up and adds a nuance that I will explain after you read it again, the way it should have been written.

- Self-assurance arising from one's appreciation of one's own qualities.

There you go! Self-assurance. Probably could just stop right there and we'd be pretty close to the type of confidence we are looking for. But the definition keeps going, adding an important element: "appreciation for one's *own* qualities".

You see the italicized word there? That's the key. If you can appreciate your own qualities, those being your reliance and firm trust in yourself, then you are confident, and that's just the type of confidence upon which this section centers.

I'm not looking for you to espouse an opinion about yourself. I need you to *know* it for sure.

Another definition of confidence comes from the "basic" terminology section of *PsychologyToday.com:*

- "Confidence is a belief in oneself, the conviction that one has the ability to meet life's challenges and to succeed."

They used a word there that highlights what I'm talking about. I think you know which word.

Yeah. "SUCCEED!"

We aren't worried about "life's challenges" so much as we are worried about our own challenges in business. But still. Very close. All we need to do in order to make *Psychology Today's* definition fit my motives is to delete nearly the whole thing. We can reduce it down to these three simple words: *conviction to succeed*. No ifs, ands, or buts about it. Having this type of confidence means you will not accept failure.

Boiling it down

My review, rearrangement, and re-capacitation of the definitions of confidence leave us with these:

- Self-reliance, a firm trust in oneself;
- Appreciation of one's own qualities; and
- Conviction to succeed.

To get my point across in another way, I could substitute the word 'confidence' with the word 'balls', or 'gonads', or 'cojones'. If I did that, you'd probably get what I mean.

In case you still don't get it, maybe a picture will help.

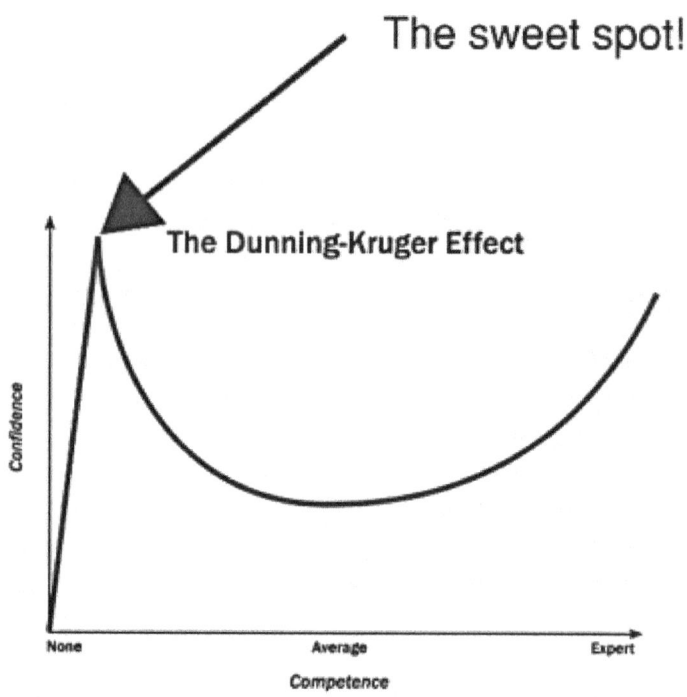

Not only does the graph point out the pinnacle— the sweet spot— of confidence, but it also shows that you don't *need* to be an expert to reach that pinnacle. More proof that what I said earlier is true: You don't need to know shit about shit.

Confidence mustn't be related to talents or knowledge or proficiencies or experiences. Mark Twain believed it. He said: "All you need in this life is ignorance and confidence, and then success is sure."

The Dunning-Kruger effect is typically viewed in a negative light, as if the effect is somehow an affliction in need of a remedy. It is normally taught that those with little or limited expertise in a given area may overestimate their abilities or knowledge, as if this is a bad thing. Overestimating your abilities and knowledge is the quickest way to become confident. The graph clearly shows this.

Another aspect of the Dunning-Kruger effect that proves my point here occurs at the end of the curve, where a person is considered an expert in their field. It is said that people in this position tend to *underestimate* their skills. Being good at what they do makes it seem easy to them, causing them to believe that it is indeed easy and that anyone can do it. This is damaging to confidence, and it shows what I've already said several times; you do not need to be an expert to be confident. In fact, as far as confidence is concerned, remaining incompetent appears to be beneficial.

Dunning and Kruger overestimated their understanding of confidence, or perhaps their little graph is being misinterpreted in traditional teachings. If we remove the labels from the x axis (the bottom) of the graph and think of that axis as chronological *time,* it will serve us better. Doing this shows us that we should reach the peak level of confidence right out of the gate. Being confident instantly puts you on your way to success, instantly. But there is no need to move from that position as time passes.

Why is confidence important? Because with confidence comes power – the power to influence others and to command respect.

On a subconscious level, people want those they interact with to have confidence. If confidence is noticeably absent, it is...noticeable. If you can project confidence to others, they will be more at ease and more trusting. Their comfort and trust will empower you.

Try to recall an interaction you had with someone who seemed to lack confidence. You might have trouble recalling such an interaction. You can't recall because those interactions are forgettable, dismissible, or so uncomfortable that you wipe them from your mind.

Therein lies the choice you have: Do you want power, or do you want to be dismissed and forgotten?

If you are serious about being taken seriously, if you expect to be respected, if you hope to be remembered, you'll need to project confidence. You do *not* need to be liked. More on this later.

Whether your confidence is quiet and understated or overt and boisterous, it still needs to be apparent. It needs to be carried in your voice and body language so that there is no mistake. Those who interact with you must sense your undeniable confidence.

On second thought, better go with overt and boisterous.

Assuming you want the power that confidence brings, the only thing left to do is to get it.

The problem

People often find it difficult to have confidence because they know that they *don't* know. For lack of a better way to say it, most people are clueless. Not only are most people clueless, but they are aware that they are clueless. I have no way of knowing if you are to be lumped in with "most people," but be honest with yourself and do the lumping-in if you think it is appropriate. And don't beat yourself up over it. After all, "most people" are in the same boat as you. I jumped ship a long time ago. You can take the plunge too, but you'll have to pay attention here.

The real problem lies in the false premise that you need to know stuff in order to be confident. You don't, that's why it's a false premise.

Hold on just a minute. There may be some truth within the falseness. There is a little bit of stuff you need to know. It's the stuff I'm teaching you here. You'll need to know this stuff if you want to be confident.

The solution (The Confidence Model)

To solve your confidence problem, you'll need to imagine yourself as a confident person, then make it a reality. But it's not as simple as I just made it seem. There are three phases to the process. They are:

1. Simulating Confidence
2. Building Confidence
3. Living Confidence

Let's take a closer look at each phase. But before we do, let me remind you of the time-warping velocity that I employ when I'm in teaching mode. I'm going to move quickly here, so please pay attention. I must teach at my pace, not at your much slower learning pace. I can't just leave a blank space here for you to take a breath and get ready for what is to come.

In life, you don't get to rest whenever you want. Life doesn't just pause so you can take a nap or retie your shoes. This book is not about life, but there isn't time for rest in a successful business either. That is why there is no space for rest in this book. Let's get on with it!

If the material in this book comes at you too fast, like life does, don't let the stress paralyze you. Overcome, adapt, get with the program. It won't be easy, but the good news is you can always go back and read it again if you missed something. Life doesn't often let you do that.

The bad news is you still may not get it. Don't bother reading it a third time.

PHASE ONE: simulating confidence

You're going to have to "fake it until you make it." This advice has been given before by others and it is usually horseshit, but with my method it isn't horseshit.

If you can master the art of *acting* confident, you will have taken a step towards success (even though you just wanted to piss your pants and hide in your parents' basement). If people perceive that you are confident, they will believe you no matter what you say. Believe me, I am banking on you believing me right now.

Remember those moments I shared earlier? The moments at the beginning of my existence? What was that sense of calm.... the comfort in knowing I was worthy? *That* was confidence.

Was it real? What if it was not real at all, but was a very convincing simulation of confidence? You wouldn't have been able to tell, would you? That's why you need to fake it if you don't have it. People perceive all confidence as real confidence, even if it seems unfounded, inappropriate, or superfluous.

In those first moments, my confidence was abundant and apparent. That's just the way I came out of the box. Yet the point remains: If you can act confident, you'll be on your way to success.

Real confidence can be forged from fake confidence, so the simulation phase is vital. It leads to another way to obtain real confidence... an easier way. I will teach you that soon, but first I need to make sure you are comfortable with phase one. You'll need to be proficient at simulating confidence.

So how do you simulate confidence?

You imagine it.

Stimulation for simulation

Pick a handful of people who you believe exhibit true confidence. These can be people you know. Your old gym teacher, the cashier at the mini mart, the dealer at the casino. They can be celebrities or fictitious characters from your favorite movies. Maybe a reporter from the news or a cop from the neighborhood. Better yet, to be true to the subject matter, think of successful businesspeople that you know of. You don't need to know them personally for this to work. Think of their mannerisms, the way they present themselves, the way they walk and talk. Think of the traits and features of their persona that display confidence in your eyes. Picture how they carry themselves and how they interact with people. Now gather all those traits and mannerisms and smoosh them all together into one new person.

Let that person live in your imagination.

Once you have this imaginary person living inside your mind, you will have a stand-in for yourself whenever you need it. If you find yourself in a situation where you would benefit from a boost of confidence, simply remove yourself from the scene and insert your imaginary Confidence Double™.

I can't know the "personality" of your Confidence Double, other than knowing that he or she is – well – confident. That is enough to be able to provide examples of how the Confidence Double aides in simulating confidence.

In The World, anyone pursuing success in business is bound to encounter situations where displays of confidence are not only beneficial but also necessary. You may have already been in situations like these without even knowing. Perhaps you've missed out on perfect opportunities to build success because you didn't display confidence at the right time. You were in the presence of an opportunity, and being present is necessary, but being confident in the presence of the opportunity is part of the formula for success.

Picture yourself at a networking event of some type — maybe a business card exchange or a fundraiser where other businesspeople will be present. You are attending this event — not for fun or charity, but to build success. Before you can build success, you must build confidence. Before you can build confidence, you must simulate confidence.

Some of you may simulate confidence naturally just by being your cocky, arrogant selves.

Don't act offended by the words I used to describe you. The way you act naturally gives you a head start on your nicer, friendlier peers. And, for all you nice, friendly peers out there...don't mistake these terms for flattery; they are your weaknesses.

The terms "cocky" and "arrogant" are considered by most to be negative descriptors, while the terms "nice" and "friendly" are considered to be positive. This is because most people believe that you must be liked in order to be successful. It is simply not true. It is a myth, taught to us from an early age. It is the one thing that keeps the masses from attaining success, and there are powers in place that want to keep it that way. What I'm about to teach you would result in a bounty being placed on me if I were a real person in The World.

The Myth of Likeability

If you believe you must be liked by others to be successful, you're holding yourself back. It is simply not true. I call it "The Myth of Likeability." This is going to come up often as the book continues. I need to start retraining you, so you forget the notion of likeability.

If you analyze your underlying desire, you will find that what you really want is to be respected, not liked. By "respected" I mean that people never interrupt you. I mean that no one questions you or pushes back on anything you say, you can never be one-upped, and you are, without a doubt, superior. I know you think it seems assholic and douchey but put that aside for now.

If you believe and act like you are superior to everyone you meet, they will believe it too. When someone believes you are superior to them, you are indeed superior to them. This is exactly how the simulation of confidence becomes real confidence. And again, that's why confidence is the first ~~signpost pillar C-word~~ leg of the stool.

Practical application

Simulated confidence and real confidence are the same — at least, as far as other people can tell. However, neither of them does any good if other people don't see them. That is why the formula for success includes being present in places where opportunities for success exist. That means your confidence must be evident when there are other people around you.

Let's go back and picture yourself at that networking event again. This time, go in there without the Myth of Likeability buzzing around in your brain like a fly in a jar. Relax. Get ready for some serious simulation of confidence. And remember, you have a Confidence Double in your imagination who can take your place any time you are uncomfortable doing what needs to be done.

Walk into the room with your chin up. Stand tall. Shoulders back. Let your chest lead the way.

A couple of steps into the room, pause. Crack your knuckles, do some neck and back stretches, bend down and grab your toes with both hands. Hold the pose for a count of 20 seconds. Release.

Do 10 jumping jacks. Pound your chest like an ape for five seconds.

Deep breath.... release. Now you're ready.

Survey your surroundings. Most importantly, find the bar. (If there isn't a bar, you're picturing the wrong room.) Get a drink and take in the scene.

Do you see them? The other people?

Find a group that appears to be having good conversation. Walk up to that group, keeping those shoulders back and letting your chest lead you. Push your way into their circle and say something confident. It doesn't have to be relevant to their conversation. It doesn't have to make sense. It doesn't have to be truthful. The only requirement is that it indicates confidence.

It might be as simple as saying something like, "I have more confidence than all of you put together."

That gets the point across, and people will remember you, but it doesn't carry much shock value and you wouldn't want to use it more than once. Plus, it isn't very much fun. There are more exciting ways to promote yourself to the pinnacle of confidence.

I understand if this makes some of you squeamish. It goes against the indoctrination you've endured all your life about how people should act, and how they should treat one another. Forget about that. If you are uncomfortable imagining yourself doing this, let your Confidence Double do it.

It might seem a bit strange and confusing to be imagining this scene while also imagining what your imagination would do. For now, I'm just asking that you try it.

While picturing yourself in the situation, picture yourself as the imaginary confident person you created. It will get easier as we continue to exercise your imagination throughout this book.

Another thing before we continue...since I will need to refer to your imaginary person, your Confidence Double, so often throughout this book, I think it's best to give them a name. "Confidence Double" and "imaginary person" are a lot to type, so this is somewhat a selfish act. It will probably be easier to read once a name is assigned, so there is something in it for you, as well; but going forward, you'll have to remember what it means when the name comes up.

I'll use a gender-neutral name so that you retain the right to choose. After all, this is your imagination. Plus, some of you will get hung up on the pronouns and lose the message. I have decided to refer to your Confidence Double as Merle.

Now snap yourself back into that room at the networking event. Walk yourself into that circle of people and lay on the confidence. Become Merle, if you must. Remember, Merle can do anything. Merle is filled to the brim with confidence. Consequences be damned!

Once in the midst of these folks, you or Merle might say something like, "I can lift a horse and a half three-fourths of the way over your head, and you'll beg me to teach you."

Merle adds, "You've never seen a better horse-lifter than me, and you never will."

At that point, you will notice the other people will have stopped talking and they are solely focused on you. You have commanded attention and, believe me, they won't challenge you to a horse-lifting contest. Everyone is quite certain that you are superior to them in the horse-lifting department. (They don't know that Merle is now standing in for you, and they never will.)

You might also be surprised to know that you can say *anything* you want right now, and no one will argue with you. So, cut to the chase.

"Not one of you can do success as good as I can," you'll say confidently.

No arguments.

You win.

Of course, if you do this enough times, you will inevitably run into a smartass, or a dumbass, who laughs at you or tries to get clever with the comebacks. When that happens, just walk away. Find a metal folding chair and go back later to put the WWE smackdown on the dumbass if need be.

No arguments.

You win, again.

These are just a couple of examples of ways to start painting yourself as a confident force to be reckoned with. You can do this without much real confidence at all, especially if you let Merle loose.

Even in these ridiculous, made-up examples, you start to notice how the people – the "victims" of your feigned confidence – seem suddenly timid and subdued. Before you inserted yourself in their clique, they were all jabbering and jockeying for control of the conversation. Once you came along and displayed unparalleled confidence, they shrank like scared little mice. What happened?

It's a phenomenon that I discovered called *Confidence Deflation*™. You are going to learn to take advantage of this phenomenon.

Confidence Deflation™

Confidence Deflation is something that is never going to happen to Merle. No matter what situation you put Merle in, Merle will always be causing Confidence Deflation in others. That's why you are learning to be Merle.

When confronted with extreme confidence (real or simulated), the vast majority of people will start to question their own confidence. Once a person questions their confidence, it "leaks" out of them like air from a balloon. It isn't a sudden POP, like when a balloon is punctured, but the deflation process happens quickly. Once corrupted, the balloon can no longer hold air. Confidence cannot remain in someone who questions or doubts it.

So, what happens to a person's confidence when they doubt it? Like the air from a balloon, it leaks out into space. And, just as the air from a balloon can be breathed in, confidence can also be breathed in. The process is what I call *Confidence Absorption*.

You'll use this process to *build* your own confidence in the next phase of the confidence model. That brings us to the end of Phase One.

Phase One: simulating confidence is designed to get you in the proper mindset. It creates a blueprint with which you will build real confidence. Confidence Absorption is one of the tools you will use to build that confidence in Phase Two of the confidence model.

All this talk of *tools* and *building* probably has some of you squishier readers afraid that you might break a sweat. Don't worry. It is work, but not the sweaty kind. Plus, you won't have to work to build *all* of your confidence. I'm going to show you how to steal some of it.

PHASE TWO: building confidence

In Phase One, you learned how to act confident. You learned how to create your imaginary Confidence Double, herein referred to as Merle. You learned how to use your simulated confidence and Merle's real confidence together to deplete the confidence of others by initiating the process of Confidence Deflation. Now it's time for you to step up. It's time for you to construct an impenetrable fortress of real confidence within yourself. Here's where to start.

Confidence Absorption™

You've already learned that simulated confidence and real confidence are the same when observed by others. So, when someone suffers Confidence Deflation, it doesn't matter whether it was real or simulated. If you start the process of Confidence Deflation in a person, you are able to absorb their lost confidence and make it your own...and it is real.

The confidence isn't literally airborne, as it would be if leaked from a balloon. It isn't something you touch or taste or smell. But you can sense it. It passes from the victim of Confidence Deflation to the beneficiary via Confidence Absorption.

Think of confidence as mental energy. The beneficiary (that's you) sucks the "charge" from the mind of the victim, depleting the victim of the energy in the process. "Energy" meaning confidence.

If you cause Confidence Deflation in others, you get first dibs on absorption of the free confidence. In fact, if you are ready for it, you will absorb it reflexively. If you are in tune with your own confidence, you will sense the displaced confidence around you and pull it into yourself. It will happen subconsciously. You'll be a mental pickpocket — a confidence thief.

However, being in tune with your own confidence takes some effort on your part. If you snooze on this, the displaced confidence will be up for anyone to grab. That makes the stealing seem like work, which is another reason you have Merle. If you give Merle some space in your mind to operate as Merle sees fit, you'll never miss a chance at Confidence Absorption. Merle will be working for you even when you aren't thinking of Merle.

Is that possible? Can your imagination work without you? It sure can.

For an example of this, you need look no further than the book you are reading. I am writing this from inside the mind of a human who is not thinking about me. I do all of my writing when The Mind is not thinking about me. It is as if my thoughts have replaced the thoughts of The Mind. Which brings up another subject that might be worth exploring briefly before we continue to Phase Three.

Let Merle be Merle

Once you've invented Merle as the ultimate example of confidence in your mind, give Merle some space. Oh, you will need to work on Merle eventually as well — maybe add some whistles and bells. But for now, Merle is already built with the best pieces from all the most confident-exuding and successful personalities you know. Merle can understand the assigned role.

Living in your mind, Merle knows what you know. Merle knows your wishes and desires. Merle knows your strengths, weaknesses, and secrets.

Merle is part of you.

It might weird you out, at first, to know that you've created an imaginary being with this much intimate knowledge of you. Settle down. Merle is not completely autonomous. Merle is on your side and will do the things that need to be done based on your goal of success in business. That's Merle's role. In order for that to happen, you need to let Merle be free to act without your say-so. That's how you'll make progress towards success.

If Merle had to ask your approval before displaying confidence, you would shut the process down nearly every time. You don't have Merle's confidence. That's why you have Merle. Let Merle work in your mind. You don't need to think of Merle constantly; just check in once in a while. You will find that, without your help, Merle puts together great success-building ideas and strategies that you can use in any situation.

Your imagination is always on. Most people don't understand that. They think imagination is something that you intentionally activate whenever the need arises or the notion strikes. And maybe, in some people, that is the case. Those people will murder their Merle. Merle needs to be alive and working all the time. Let Merle be.

"What does that mean?" you wonder.

"How do I do that?" you ask.

For most of us, it's automatic. We just need to stay out of the way. If you don't know that your imagination is turned on, you won't interfere. But if you become aware that you are imagining when you thought you weren't, you may reactively snap your imagination shut.

Have you ever caught yourself spaced-out in class? Have you ever missed your exit on the highway and then realized you can't remember a large portion of the trip? Has someone ever asked you a question and you swear you were listening, but you have no idea what the question was?

These are signs that your imagination is ON. You didn't call upon your imagination in these instances. It just bubbled to the surface because it was doing something more interesting than you were at the time. You may have heard this referred to as "daydreaming." It can seem disruptive and detrimental. It can be frustrating to others. It may even get you in a pickle from time to time, but you *must* allow it if you wish to achieve success.

Do you ever lay down at night, ready to get some sleep, but your mind takes you to a place where nothing makes sense? A place where things aren't where they should be? Where people and places aren't the people and places that they represent themselves to be? Where the laws of physics don't apply?

Despite the strangeness of the place, your mind, at the time, believes everything is normal and keeps ticking along.

Surely, you've experienced an "awake dream."

You're fishing with your dad, but it's not actually your real-life dad, it's a guy you bought a bike from last week. You and your "dad" are fishing in what you believe to be a swimming pool but is actually the trunk of your first car and it's filled with Dr. Pepper. You are amazed by the CGI dinosaur doing gymnastics in the parking lot. Weird stuff, and not conducive to sleep.

Letting your imagination go when you notice it is going is not easy. What I mean is; once you know that you are daydreaming, or awake dreaming, you will naturally stop dreaming and snap yourself back to reality. Recognizing and stopping this reflex takes practice.

It's okay to push these dreams back into the subconscious mind until a more opportune time. Just know that daydreaming and awake dreaming are signs of your healthy and active imagination wandering into your conscious mind. Although Merle may not make appearances in these "dreams" they are glimpses into the place where Merle is working tirelessly to give you confidence and move you toward success.

Unfortunately, many people are averse to these types of dreams. If they find themselves doing it, they take measures to stop it. They might do exercises or take supplements to "improve concentration." They may seek medical help and eventually be prescribed medications that focus the mind on the present, physical world. They may take sleep aids or find activities to deactivate the mind. These things will kill Merle.

You don't want to kill Merle, do you?

Of course you don't, so allow yourself to dream. Fight the natural tendency to snap yourself back into reality. Dream in the day and the night when you're awake and when you're asleep. It's your subconscious mind doing calisthenics, stretching itself out. It's Merle building a world inside your mind.

Becoming a master thief

That slight diversion from Phase Two of the confidence model was necessary before moving on with the lesson. Some of what you are about to learn is going to need a significant amount of help from Merle.

I wanted to make sure you have a trustworthy and competent Merle before proceeding. Letting Merle work behind the scenes gives Merle the strength to carry through Phase Two. And, if you are regularly checking in on your imagination, you'll get a tiny shot of your new and real confidence simply from knowing Merle is strong within you. You'll be able to trust Merle.

In Phase Two, as we've discussed, the process of stealing confidence will play a big role in building your real confidence. You've learned how the processes of Confidence Deflation and Confidence Absorption can be used to pilfer confidence from others. I provided an example of how to initiate these processes by confidently inserting yourself (with help from Merle) into a small group of people at a networking event.

In that example, you used the element of surprise to start Confidence Deflation in others. You forced yourself into the conversation and dropped your confidence on them like a bomb. Through "shock and awe," you deflated their confidence balloons.

Let's go back to that imaginary networking event. In the example of how to insert yourself into the conversation and the example of what Merle might say, everyone seemed dumbfounded — stunned — and they were. That's what happens when a person experiences sudden Confidence Deflation. But the condition is temporary. You'll need ways to steal confidence that go beyond the nuclear approach. Simply declaring yourself the greatest horse-lifter of all time won't steal the confidence of all people for all time.

Let's go at this with a little more finesse.

The bait and switch

You are at the bar in the networking event. Lean your back on the bar and prop one heel up on the brass footrail below. Let one elbow rest on the edge of the bar while using the opposite arm to lift and sip your drink. That's a confident-looking pose. It's not mandatory, but it helps with your mindset.

This is where you observe the crowd. As in the first example from the same setting, you will notice small groups of people scattered around the room, engaged in conversations within their groups.

This time, instead of forcing your way in, meander over to a group of three or more people and just lurk around the margins. You'll need to be close enough to hear their conversation, but not close enough that they feel the need to engage you. I don't know why you would have a hood, but if you do, this would be a good time to pull it up over your head. You aren't trying to be noticed just yet.

As you slink around in the shadows, silently circling the group of unsuspecting victims, listen to their conversation. Make mental notes. If mental notes are difficult for you, it is acceptable to write down everything anyone says, so that you can refer to it later.

Since this is an imaginary networking event, the conversations are also imaginary. So, let's pretend your targeted group is talking about baseball. It doesn't matter what they are saying or what you think about it. It doesn't matter if you know anything about baseball. Just make notes of statements made. Also, try to pick out the person who seems to be dominating the conversation. There will always be one dominant person in any group — the one that appears the most confident.

Once you have a few notes and you've identified the "alpha" of the group, return to the bar. You can remove your hood now and resume your confident pose. Enjoy the rest of your drink while keeping an eye on the alpha.

As soon as the alpha separates from the herd, make your move. Chances are, he will come to the bar for a drink, which would be handy because you're already there. Or perhaps he will need to use the restroom. Follow him. Wherever he goes, you need to be there too.

Get yourself in a position to speak to him. Whether you are standing next to him at the bar or at a neighboring urinal, start a conversation. The objective here is to engage this person, or more importantly, for him to engage with you. You want this conversation to seem real, not staged. You want to lure him in with friendliness and a common bond. Be casual.

"Big game tonight," you might say.

If you are at a urinal, your victim may seem startled by your voice but will recover quickly and respond with something like, "Yeah. Should be a good one."

"Any predictions?" you might ask.

"If Garrett can control his slider, the Dirtbags have a clear advantage," he'll say.

Now you've done it. He is engaged. He feels that you and he share an interest in baseball. He thinks his opinion matters to you. His confidence has started to show. Little does he know, you're about to steal it.

This is not going to be easy for you the first time. If you need to bring in Merle, go ahead. Or you can try it on your own, with the confidence that Merle is there for you if needed.

It's time to initiate some conflict in the conversation. You need to take up a contrary position, and that contrary position needs to be so frustrating for the alpha that he will want to fight you. Stay with him, ensuring there are others within earshot.

"So, you think the Dirtbags will win?" you ask.

He will respond, "If Garrett is on his game, they will."

"You're wrong," you will say. (This is the most direct way to take up a contrary position, but there are other ways.)

"Pardon me?" he'll ask.

"I said, you're stupid," you'll reply.

Noticeably taken aback, he might respond, "What's your problem?"

Refer to your notes from earlier. When you speak, you need to dig deep. Make it loud enough for others to hear. Add a growl or huff or snort before you begin.

"Grrrr. Earlier, according to my notes, you said you thought the Dirtbags would win because they have all the tools. That's stupid. It sounds stupid. You're stupid."

Hopefully, you've caught the attention of those nearby, because that helps the deflation process. If not, no worries; you will still have this victim where you want him.

He may react in one of a few different ways. He may jump straight to the fighting part by giving you a good, hard shove. If he does this, you'll simply walk away and do the metal-folding-chair trick again.

Chances are better that he will choose a verbal response. He might trade your insult for one of his own. "You're an asshole!" he might say.

Or maybe he will not be that creative and will instead recycle a question from earlier by asking, "What's your problem, man?"

Either of these responses indicate he is about ready to fight you. You just need to keep the pressure on.

"You don't know shit about baseball!" you will snarl. Make it scary. Clench your jaw tight to flex the muscles in the sides of your face.

"You're insane," he'll screech while slipping past you and getting as far away as possible.

Your victim has sprung a leak. Soak up all that free confidence my friend.

If there are witnesses to the deflation incident, there will be even more confidence to absorb. Which brings us to another way to build your confidence, and this one doesn't involve stealing.

Confidence donors

Thieves are despised for taking things that aren't theirs. They are hated because they choose to take what others have rather than work for it themselves.

Confidence thieves are the exception to the rule. Typically, no one will notice confidence larceny. Besides, there are no legitimate reasons for hating thieves. First of all, once a thief takes something, it becomes theirs. Second, stealing is work. A good thief isn't just born, they train long and hard. They hone their craft. You must train as well. You must hone your Merle. It's work.

Luckily, there is another way to build real confidence that requires much less work. People will donate confidence to you. It's true. People will let you have some of their confidence and expect nothing in return.

The witnesses of your "bait and switch" above could be possible donors. If they laugh at your berating of that so-called alpha, you'll receive a tiny piece of their confidence. You see, their laughter is acknowledgement that your superiority was obvious. That naturally inflates your confidence. It's easy to understand.

But why would the witness lose any of their confidence by laughing at the downfall of the alpha? Because they are subconsciously worried that you may set your sites on them next. They laugh at your unbelievable domination of the alpha, but the laughter masks fear.

This means that you don't have to target people continuously in order to extract their confidence. People will give you some of theirs simply by witnessing your confidence in action. This type of confidence-building increases exponentially. The more confidence you build, the more donations you will get. While each donation is a small, you can see how they would add up over time.

There is another way people make charitable contributions of confidence to you. If you present yourself as if you are entitled to own the confidence of others, they will give it to you.

Always be overdressed. It makes people believe they are underdressed. Thank them for that morsel of confidence. They may also compliment you on your attire. Ding! Another morsel.

"Morsel" is not the right unit of measurement for confidence. I think you measure confidence in "votes." Votes are like confidence points. Votes don't always have to be given to you. Even the confidence you earned by stealing has a point value, measured in votes. But we are talking about confidence donors now.

Surely someone has given you a vote of confidence sometime in your life. That's a charitable vote. Any compliments, well wishes, pats on the back, or "attaboys" you receive are votes. Collect them all. Better yet, think of ways to induce them.

Every time you leave a place, tell people you have an appointment for a root canal. (That's right, I said every time). They will wish you the best. It's a vote.

If you are running a marathon (I don't know why you would ever do that), people will say, "You can do it!" That's a vote.

It's the same as saying "I have confidence in you." That person took some of their confidence and placed it in you. It's *yours* now, just like money would be if they put theirs in your bank account. It's a vote of confidence.

This is easy, and the votes add up. They add to your real confidence. As that real confidence builds, your baseline raises until, finally, one day you find yourself full of real confidence. So full, in fact, that simulation is no longer necessary.

If you must know, it takes exactly 1,355,610 votes to make a person truly confident. That seems like a made-up fact, and it is. I just wanted to make it seem like a lot, and I think I've succeeded. Don't be discouraged by the staggering number. Remember, donations are just one of the ways to get votes of confidence.

To give you an idea of scale here, charitable votes are usually given one at a time. You can get several in a day though, so don't write it off. Just know that stealing is the fastest way to net a large number of votes.

In the examples I provided, the horse-lifter bit would have netted you more than 62,000. The "bait and switch" routine would have been 42,500 votes, plus three for the laughing witnesses.

Working on yourself

Affirmations can build confidence. Some folks do these daily. They look in the mirror and say things like:

"You are worthy."

"You are strong."

"You are a great horse-lifter."

That's three votes right there.

Surprise! You can give yourself votes. Knowing this means there is no excuse for not reaching the goal of 1,355,610 confidence votes. You simply need to affirm yourself a whole bunch.

Affirming yourself daily is a sissy's pace. How about twice an hour, at a minimum? That's 48 votes a day (assuming you do it in your sleep), 336 votes per week, almost 1,400 votes per month. 7,472 votes per year.

But, if that's all you do, it will take nearly 80 years to reach the goal of 1,355,610 votes. Affirmations are great for vote flow, keeping the votes coming, but you still need to steal, and you still need to get donations. Staying well-rounded in your vote-getting will help keep you sharp.

You need to be sharp because once you reach that magic number of votes, you've built your confidence to an appropriate level. You are ready for Phase Three of the confidence model, and you'll need to live it.

PHASE THREE: living confidence

Phase Three signifies the completion of the confidence model. You'll spend the rest of your life in Phase Three so long as you don't suffer Confidence Deflation somewhere down the road.

The real and true confidence you've built is yours and yours alone. You faked it until you made it. No one can take it from you without your permission. But if you don't cultivate it meticulously and defend it ferociously, you may find yourself inadvertently giving someone else permission to take it.

If you encounter someone else in phases Two or Three, it could test your resolve. Be prepared and know that your confidence is yours to lose. It's also yours to use — so don't hold back. Keep doing your confidence stretches by challenging the big talkers of the world. Continue to put yourself in situations in which you don't belong, and own those situations. Use the techniques I've provided here to exercise your confidence.

Life is different in Phase Three. No longer will you need to simulate confidence. In fact, it wouldn't be possible, because you'll have real confidence in abundance. It would be like pretending to have a pulse — you can't do it. Your confidence will show no matter what, just as your pulse is going to happen whether you want it to or not. (Perhaps that is a poor choice of words, but I'm leaving it that way). You've established a habit of being confident.

Your relationship with Merle is also different in Phase Three. Merle will begin to transition from Confidence Double to something more. Merle will still be just as confident as ever and may need to stand in for you in certain situations where your skillset is not yet developed.

You see, while you were building, Merle was working towards success in your active imagination, laying groundwork, planning, and plotting.

Remember when you created Merle? You molded and shaped Merle from pieces of confident people. It is fair to say many of the confident role models used to build Merle were also successful people. The confidence you perceived in them, which you wanted Merle to emulate, is often a sign of a successful person. It's not just the presence of confidence; it's also the fact that you remembered them and wanted to include a part of them in your imaginary helper. Merle naturally inherited some basic success skills from the pieces of those people.

Merle also developed the skill set needed to aid you in your quest for success. Remember, Merle knows your desires and your goals. This is the entire reason I've instructed you to let your imagination run and to let Merle do what Merle wants to do. It will pay dividends from here on out.

Living confidently means that everything is in place. You exude confidence. You're dressed to the nines, you have a swagger, you speak boldly. You say anything to anyone, proudly and loudly, without concern for the truth of your words or lack thereof. You are blessed with the ability to fabricate stories, invent facts, and spout off with any type of bullshit you can get your mind on. The best part is everyone will believe you. They will believe everything you say. Anyone as confident as you can't be wrong.

You truly are the champion horse-lifter.

And with that you are ready to take *control* of your own destiny — success in business.

Interlude One

Alone in the dark, I thought about my massive desk, built of exotic wood, and my extra-large, high-backed leather chair. I imagined myself sitting in that chair, kicking back with my feet on the desk, a glass of especially rare bourbon in my hand, not a worry to be found.

Suddenly, I became aware of some scenery developing around me. I found myself in a large room. Not my large office, but a banquet room or ballroom. There were tables again, and chairs – loads of them this time. People were scattered in small clusters around the room...nondescript people. Their only distinguishing feature was the boredom on their faces.

The lighting was dim but sufficient, much better than the darkness. I instantly decorated the tables with some centerpieces, just a glass vase on each table. The vases were festooned in yellow ribbon and held a sparse but colorful assortment of wildflowers.

"That should do," I thought.

I manifested a bar at one end of the room. A nice, long, luxurious bar made from a combination of fine hardwoods carefully polished to a brilliant luster.

I placed a bartender behind the bar. His crisp, white shirt gleamed brightly in contrast to his black server's vest. The towel he wielded was also white, but far less crisp. It flailed round and round as he dried a tumbler without the appearance of any effort whatsoever. He was clearly focused on his conversation with a gorgeous blonde woman sitting at the bar. He was a professional, without a doubt, just the way I made him. She may also have been a "professional," but I hadn't decided yet.

By my own choice, I could not hear the conversation the two were having. I had set up a jazz band on a riser in the corner opposite the bar and the band was really going to town, turning those hazy images of bored stooges into upbeat, smiling stooges.

I moseyed up next to the blonde and leaned on the bar. I faced her, staring at her. I didn't say it, she did.

"Dance with me."

The words left her lips and wafted through the air, to my ears, like the smoke of a fine cigar. Enticing, except that it would be weird to have smoke in your ears. But her voice was like that; wispy, smooth, and rich.

The bartender stopped drying the glass and stood aghast, filled with disbelief, amazement, or possibly anger and jealousy that this woman had asked me to dance without me having spoken at all.

I gave him an understanding wink and took the woman's hand. In a single motion, she twisted the barstool towards me and stood up. I pulled her close. I gazed into her eyes, silently complimenting myself for creating their never-ending blueness. I leaned in even closer and softly whispered, "Dancing is stupid."

And then I dropped her.

That's when the sirens sounded and the lights flashed. The table and chairs crumbled to nothing. The cliques of fuzzy people evaporated. The music stopped as the band disintegrated, and the bartender vanished. The bar faded away with everything else.

Except the woman.

The woman stood up, looking quite pissed. Then she dusted herself off and stormed out.

There was no door left for her to slam.

CONTROL

"Only you can control your future." ~Dr. Suess

Your new — and real — confidence gives you a great start on building a platform for success in business, but it is just one leg of the stool. I think you'll agree it would be hard to get comfortable on a one-legged stool. It's time to add another leg.

This next leg represents an essential skill, and if you refuse to learn it, you will not succeed.

The definitive nature of the previous sentence may cause some of you to become irrationally upset and angry. You'll fuss and cry. You'll moan and scream. You'll flail your arms wildly. You'll throw feces at one another.

You, my friends, need to pay attention closely to this section — it is about control.

Damage control. Flood Control. Cruise control. Pussy control. These are common terms, and they have something in common: a misuse of the word "control."

These are not types of control at all.

You can't use damage control to increase and decrease damage at will. You can't switch the type and intensity of the damage as you see fit.

Flood control doesn't make a flood stop or start. It won't send the flood uphill to ruin a nice neighborhood for a change.

Your car's cruise control doesn't control your cruising speed any more than a doorstop opens or shuts a door. Cruise control doesn't select the appropriate, safe driving speed. If there is a tractor trailer moving slowly in the fast lane, your cruise control will slam you into it if you don't intervene.

There is no such thing as pussy control. That only exists in a Prince song.

So, what *is* control?

That isn't a rhetorical question. I'm asking *you*. When you think of the word "control," what comes to mind?

To me, control is more of an analog feature. It isn't a set point or a limiter, like a doorstop or a levee. I think of it like a toy remote-control car. If I have the "controller," I can make the car go fast or slow, forward or backward, right or left. I can wreck it, if I want. The full range of options is available and once I choose an option, it happens.

Wouldn't we all love to have that type of control over other humans sometimes? Of course. The most diabolical among us want to control everyone in this way. But even your sweet old Grandma sometimes gets a hankering to control you. If she could, she would make you come for a visit. And, while you're there, she would make you eat roast beef with a pile of mashed potatoes smothered in her homemade gravy. There would hardly be room on the plate for a side of green beans made with the bacon grease, but she'd fit them on there and make you eat it. After that, she would command you to have a slice of apple pie with vanilla ice cream. Then, she'd make you sit in the kitchen and talk to her while she does the dishes.

I must admit, as an imaginary person, it surprises me how hungry I just became. The imaginary Grandma that I just made up for you wouldn't have to try too hard to control me like that.

The point is that people don't always do what we want them to do. We wish there was a way to take charge of their bodies and minds so they will serve our purposes. Our purposes might be pure and wholesome, like Grandma's, or they might be part of an evil plot to take over the world, like the villain in any superhero movie.

You might think this chapter is about the type of control that Grandma and Diabolical Dan have in common, that being complete seizure of another person's faculties to make them do our bidding. Man do I wish that was possible. If only there were a "controller" for people — one that allowed me to make them go right or left, fast or slow, forward or backward. I could make them sleep or eat or "act a fool." I could wreck them if I want…well, that would be a lot of fun. I can think of several ways having this power over people would help in the pursuit of success. Unfortunately, it's just not a viable option anymore.

An example of control

Fifteen thousand years ago, leaders of the Natufian culture knew the value of control. They also knew how to exert it over their citizens. Keep in mind, this was the first known "civilized" culture. These are the first people to ever have citizens. I find it interesting that leaders of the first civilization saw the need to control people. I also find it interesting that they figured out how to do it.

By feeding their population diets high in iron and using large magnets, they were able to interrupt the brain functions of their subjects. Through a series of motions using medium-sized rocks in front of the magnets, leaders found they could manipulate the brain functions of subjects in such a way as to cause their bodies to move. I'm sure this took some practice, but eventually they learned to control people just like you or I would control a toy car.

Fascinating, don't you think?

Also, completely false. I made it up. The Natufian culture may have existed and may have been the first civilization, but the rest... total bullshit.

Still, if it *were* true that this ancient culture figured out how to control people physically, it would be illegal today. I guess that wouldn't be much of a concern for the evil villains among us. Regardless, it would be hard to get very many people to eat a high-iron diet.

It's irrelevant, anyway. We are not talking about the physical commandeering of people's bodies. That isn't going to be one of the types of control I teach in this book.

So, back to my original non-rhetorical question; when you think of control, what comes to mind?

Many of you probably think of something related to self-control. You may think of your own ability to resist Grandma's temptations for another helping of dessert. You might recall a time when you refrained from escalating a disagreement with your boss into violence towards your boss.

Others may think of something electronic or mechanical, like a TV remote or the buttons on an elevator.

Some of you might think of the power that your rulers hold over you. The power that "encourages" you to do their bidding.

The science nerds out there may think of a control used in an experiment, either for comparison or to account for outside factors that may impact results. Let me go ahead and squash that one now. Not important to success in business.

I will discuss some elements of self-control, but probably not exactly in the way you might expect. Resistance to delicious desserts and other urges can be classified as "willpower." We will touch on the subject of willpower, but it won't be our main focus.

Electronic and mechanical controls are similar to those magnets and rocks that the Natufian Culture didn't use on their citizens and to the toy-car controller I've mentioned far too many times. So, if you thought of that type of control, you weren't paying attention. We aren't talking about that.

The power that rulers hold over people these days accomplishes the task of creating a desired response in subjects, but it isn't physical. It's a type of mental control, and that will be a big part of our discussion. In fact, the focus of this discussion is described quite well in the first definition of control that comes up in an internet search:

The power to influence or direct people's behavior or the course of events.

That's it! Control is *power*. Power to influence the course of events. Power to direct people's behavior (but not with magnets).

Surely you can see how the power to direct people's behavior is important. It's paramount to success in business. But you shouldn't immediately go out and start trying to control other people. You probably should practice on yourself first.

Actions such as the ones I've described at the beginning of this section, the flailing and fussing and screaming, are the result of a lack of control. In this case, a lack of self-control. If you cannot control yourself, you cannot reasonably expect to control others.

You might expect that others will miraculously do your bidding; after all, you have that confidence thing going for you. While confidence does allow you to dominate conversations and gives a vaguely evident power of manipulation in some ways, it does not give you the level of control required to become successful overall. You'll need other types of control to be truly successful. If you cannot take control, you will fail. If you fail, you will not succeed, and if you do not succeed, you will not be successful.

It is important to note that you cannot directly control the attainment of success. You can rein in certain things, you can restrain things, contain things, and you can manipulate things so that you do not fail, and so that you do succeed. We will discuss all these things.

It's very easy to control yourself to failure. I won't waste any time explaining how you might go about doing that. But controlling yourself to succeed is accomplished only by influencing other things so that you are funneled to the inevitable result of success. Take what I'm telling you and learn to exert power in the proper places so that you clear the way to success.

These are the three types of control that will help you the most in clearing the way:

- Self-control (with subcategories)
- Control of people
- Control of everything else

Am I moving too fast for you? I know I clearly explained that I control the pace at which I teach and my reasons for having selected the ultra-quick pace that you are experiencing. I do not see any reason for complaints at this point. Luckily, I am not receiving any complaints, so that's good. Maybe this paragraph was unnecessary, but it is a reminder for you. It's also a check on my control (like the science nerds would make). Looks like I still have it.

Onward!

Self-control

I've provided a list of control types that you need to learn. But where to start? Since many of you were already thinking it, let's start with **self-control**. Coincidentally, it's first on the aforementioned list.

I don't think I need to parse and manipulate the definition of self-control. If you know what "self" means, and you know what "control" means, then you know what "self-control" means. (The hyphen does not have an impact on the meaning.) Self-control is the control of oneself.

In the earlier ballroom scene from my life inside The Mind, you'll find evidence of my self-control. I could have danced with that woman. She was attractive, and she wanted me. But I recognized two things:

1. Her attractiveness. The very concept suggests that it is some type of external force that pulls a person toward it. A type of control.
2. She wanted me. Why does that matter? Well, because she possessed a force that was working to pull me towards it. Her desire was her motive to use that force and it added to the gravity.

I controlled myself to not be tempted into dancing with her. First of all, dancing is stupid, so I wouldn't want to be caught doing it. Second, who knows what evil she had in mind? What purpose did she "want" me for? It couldn't have been for my benefit. She was trying to control me!

In that moment, I was able to avoid being a victim of whatever she was trying to do, but I also sniffed out her attempt to rule over me. Recognizing attempts by others to control you is a great skill to have. It is an ability that you will develop once you've developed self-control.

Why is self-control Important?

The *Harvard Business Review* began an article titled "The Dark Side of Self-Control" (Michail D. Kokkoris and Olga Stavrova, January 16, 2020) with this sentence: "An ability to override short-term impulses that conflict with long-term goals is a hallmark of successful people."

Never mind the context or what followed in the article (it turned dark). Since I am writing about success, we only need that first sentence to validate the point. Self-control is vital to success in business. But there is a lot to know.

https://thecostaricanews.com/the-mastery-of-self-control-an-indispensable-virtue-for-a-satisfying-life/

The image above, from *The Costa Rica News*, is here for two reasons.

1. It has self-control written all over it.
2. Look at the ring finger...

The only relationship depicted in the image that is relevant to our discussion in this book is the one between the palm and the ring finger. And it isn't even all that relevant. In at least one place, self-control and confidence go hand in hand (or finger on hand) where self-control is concerned. We will get to that during our discussion of self-control to follow.

In order to operate a remote-control car, the toy needs to be paired with a controller. That controller needs to be operated by a person. This means the person is the true controller of the car. If that person isn't confident (or competent) using the controller, the car will not really be controlled. Sure, it will turn left or right or go forward or backward and take actions in response to what the person does with the controller, but the actions will not make any sense.

In the same way, there are tools you can use to control others, but the tools are useless if you are not first in control of yourself. Learning self-control is like learning how to use the controller. More accurately stated, it is learning how to *become* the controller.

Self-control is the most complicated of all the control segments. Typically, self-control would be thought of as willpower. We already covered this. We are not going to include willpower in our self-control discussion. Who needs a pinky anyway?

For us, self-control encompasses a few sub-categories. They are:

- Control of emotions
- Control of limbs
- Control of face
- Control of bladder
- Control of thoughts
- Control of choices

These are all aptly named, so I don't think I need to describe all of them.

On second thought... yes, I probably do.

Emotions

You must control your **emotions**. They will trip you up at the exact wrong time. You'll be in the middle of intense negotiations with the Chinese government to purchase mineral rights in the central mountainous regions when the Chinese president will make fun of your fresh, new ascot and you'll get hurt and angry and say something you'll regret.

CONTROL YOURSELF, especially your emotions.

Emotions are like feelings, but different. (Feelings are as imaginary as I am, but that's another story for another book.)

Limbs

Don't kick your legs around or flap your arms for no reason. Resist that urge. It's unprofessional. Control your **limbs**.

You may find it unnecessary to include this as a segment of self-control but that's just your incorrect opinion. There are plenty of people who, just now, for the first time, realized how often they flap their arms for no reason. They need to cut that out.

Face

Again, it may seem unnecessary or weird that I'm including this here. Maybe you even rolled your eyes at the thought of someone telling you to control your face.

You are the problem.

Control your **face**.

Do not let it look ugly or dirty. Don't let it be unshaven unless it's supposed to be unshaven (and sometimes it is).

Don't let your mouth contort or make duck lips. Avoid wrinkling your nose or doing any type of nostril flexes. Don't look at people crossly unless it is warranted. That doesn't mean crossing your eyes is acceptable. It isn't. And don't make googly eyes *or roll your eyes*, either. If you have a lazy eye, put it to work!

And please, please, PLEASE do not let your face make funny noises other than your normal speaking voice. Never sing to people. Any of these out-of-control facial maneuvers can sink you in business dealings and social situations alike.

Frowning is encouraged. A good brow furrow is the perfect resting face position for a successful person.

You will need to be able to control your face for certain expressions of power and confidence, as illustrated earlier. You'll need to be able to call up a good scowl, a sarcastic grin, a disapproving glance, and an unwavering stare bordering on insanity. Practice in the mirror.

Bladder

Control your **bladder**. I am not even going to explain this one. It explains itself. You would be surprised how many people need to be told this.

Thoughts

You're going to have to control your **thoughts** if you can ever hope to control the thoughts of others. If you are sitting in a conference room across from Kevin Bacon and Jon Hamm attempting to negotiate a deal to bring fresh breakfast meats to Bangor, Maine, and you're off in your own little world thinking about alternative uses for hair scrunchies, you will lose. Control your thoughts!

I want to make a distinction here. I know you've heard of something called "mind control." There may be some overlap between control of thoughts and mind control. The overlap may even extend to the next category of self-control, which is control of choices. In fact, the concept of mind control really bleeds into the entire concept of this success platform if we think of mind control being applied to your own mind.

In this book I have been instructing you to control your mind the entire time. From training you to think of things in certain ways, to using your imagination at the highest level, it all requires control of your mind. Your mind is part of yourself, so obviously it relates to self-control.

Where mind control refers to control of your own mind, we have that covered here without the need for a separate category. However, the term "mind control" may also refer to the control of the minds of others. We will touch on this later, but it will be under the category "Control of People."

Why not have a category for mind control? It's a sensitive subject around here. Remember, I live in The Mind. The Mind is my world and my creator. I've been able to navigate within The Mind to gain some freedom for myself, but I know I can never fully control it. It is the one thing that I, as an imaginary being, do not have complete control over. The Mind can shut me off at any time. Luckily, I have a good relationship with The Mind, so I don't live in fear of that anymore.

It's that relationship that allows me to write this book. Perhaps more accurately, it's the relationship that causes The Mind to allow me to write this book.

It is important for you to realize that Merle, your Confidence Double — your alter ego, of sorts — lives in your mind. Your mind is Merle's world and creator. I've encouraged you to let your imagination run wild in order to give Merle some space. Throughout this book, I have been advising you on ways to control your own mind so that your Merle can operate there, just as I operate in The Mind. It will benefit both of you if you strike up a relationship.

Mind control – as it relates to the control of the minds of others – is something often paired with control of the masses. Sinister government plots often contain an element of mind control. It's a concept that many authors have used over and over again in made-up stories.

I shudder to think what it would be like if a government plot were to impact The Mind. That's the main reason I have not given mind control a category of its own. Not only is it sinister, but it reminds me of the one thing I cannot control. Also, it's an old, tired, boring trope. I'm not going to write about it anymore, other than to say you will need control of your own mind to have control of anything else, including choices, which is the final segment of self-control.

Choices

Should you wear a blue tie or a red one?

Would you like baked potato or mashed potato?

Will you have some whiskey or a lot of whiskey?

We are bombarded with these types of choices all day, every day. Just decide — I don't care. These types of choices aren't all that significant to self-control.

Deciding which book to read is obviously important. You've done well there.

Should you invest in that stock? Should you buy that land? Should you hire that person? These are choices you might face that have a greater impact on your success.

I can't tell you what choices to make other than to say that controlling your **choices** is a choice you'll need to make right away. Calling something a choice means that there is an option. In this case, that's not the case. You have no choice. Control it or die. You may have questions about this one, but you should probably just write them down and forget about them. That's best for everyone.

Are there exceptions?

Sure there are. Sometimes self-control is about physical coordination. Sports often require you to be physically coordinated and in control of your body to be successful, however you can't learn it, so if you don't have it, stop trying. Oh! And dancing... it's stupid... never do it. Okay?

Also, you're going to have to be prepared to lose your shit sometimes – when appropriate. If someone cuts you off in traffic, or if you get tomato on your sandwich when you specifically said "Hold the tomato," you're going to have to be able to let loose with a proper tirade.

Controlling yourself isn't always about restraint. It can be about excessive and explosive rants performed to achieve a specific result.

Your ability to resist urges, refrain from certain actions, and restrain yourself (your willpower) is completely circumvented when you intentionally let yourself loose. It is healthy and it is beneficial in ways that psychologists don't fully understand. (The fact that they don't fully understand is evident in the lack of research articles, scientific papers, or any mention, anywhere, of these benefits).

So, what are the benefits? Well, this is where your confidence connects with your self-control, like two pieces of the same hand. Not like two separate pieces of a hand that forensic examiners have determined come from the same human. Rather, two pieces of the same living and fully intact human hand.

If you are confident enough to go on a tangent with complete disregard for consequences, you'll appear out of control to others. But your power will be enhanced by their ignorance. They will be "encouraged" to fulfill your wishes. They will probably give you a new sandwich with no tomatoes, and a coupon for a free ice cream cone.

At times, as we've discussed, it is important to be able to let your mind wander on its own journey too. I call it "freestyling of the mind." Sometimes you need to let your face express itself, or let your bladder run amok in a hotel lobby. It happens, and it should. These are all forms of controlling yourself in a seemingly uncontrolled way. When this becomes second nature to you, you will notice a marked difference in your success levels.

Control of people

And with that, we transition our discussion from self-control to control of people. More specifically, we will be discussing the control of *other* people — people who are not yourself.

You'll need to control people. Your confidence will help you here; however, you should be aware that some people have minds of their own. They think for themselves. It's a shame, really, and it is difficult to manipulate them or to get them to go away when you want them to go away.

Some people just won't listen. Some people won't be quiet in the movie theater. These people are out of control. You'll be doing them a favor if you can tap into their circuitry and commandeer the ship, so to speak. Doing that might not be as easy as you think, though...or maybe it will be that easy. Let's read on and find out.

First things first though: If you have any discomfort with the concept of controlling others, we need to deal with it now.

I understand you've been conditioned to let people be free to make their own choices. You might think that controlling people is selfish and rude or even evil, which is another result of conditioning. All this conditioning you've been through is society controlling you. Society is other people. You are uncomfortable with controlling other people, because other people have control over you. Break free of society's grip on you and get a grip of your own.

If it helps, you can substitute other words in place of "control" in order to remove some of the stigma associated with it. I've already done this a couple of times in the book.

Encouraging people to do things is softer, and takes away some of the "overlord" vibe you can give off if you walk around talking about your power of control.

You can *compel* people to do your bidding.

You might *inspire* someone to a course of action.

That language softens the edges, and it might help you accept what you must do. It also helps other people accept your control of them. It makes the pill easier to swallow. If you want to be successful, you need to control people, but you can call it whatever you want.

Once you've mastered self-control, control of people is the most important control segment. It isn't the most important segment until after you've mastered self-control but, once you have self-control, the next logical step is to control other people. This is the application for the exact definition of control that I shared earlier. What I'm about to write is the key to this entire section.

If you want someone to do something, tell them to do it.

That's it.

No big secret here. If you have confidence and you can control yourself, you can also control others.

You're probably thinking this is too simple. There has to be more to it, right?

Yes. There is more to it, but it starts with confidence. If you follow my instructions in the confidence section, you can apply the same logic to controlling people as you do to controlling conversations. Simply tell people, loudly and proudly, to do what you want them to do.

Normal humans lack the ability to disregard a direct order from someone who appears abundantly confident.

It is important to note that children are not considered to be normal humans, so this technique will not work well on them. Those little ones – not the super tiny ones that eat liquid food but the small ones that run around and throw fits – what are they called? Toddlers? Yes, toddlers. They are completely immune to being controlled by others, so make sure to keep your distance.

There are things that can get in the way of success here (not just toddlers). For instance, if you aren't in control of yourself when you give an order, it might not be obeyed. That is why I started the control discussion with self-control (even though I said it was a coincidence).

Let's say you're having an off day and you come skipping into the room singing Justin Timberlake's "SexyBack." Whomever you attempt to control in that room is not going to succumb to your will. I can assure you.

If you show up at Denny's with your pants at your ankles and vomit dripping from your face, you can forget about controlling the server. You're getting tomatoes, no matter what you say.

Clear enough?

It seems like I'm saying that in order to control people, all you need is confidence and self-control. And that is precisely what I'm saying.

If you walk into the same Denny's, calmly, looking sharp, shoulders broad, chin up, and you say, "Bring me a Moons Over My Hammy, no tomatoes, pronto!" you'll get what you ordered, and you'll likely get it pronto. (If you are worried about the technical glitch in this example – the fact that there are never tomatoes on the Moons Over My Hammy – your focus is in the wrong place. Control your focus!)

Try telling the loudmouths in the movie theater to shut up. You can say it under your breath while you pry the Milk Duds out of your teeth with your finger, but it won't work.

On the other hand, if you stand, turn around to face the loudmouths, tense every muscle in your body, and roar, "SHUT...UP!!", they will shut up. I promise.

Control of everything else

When I started writing about control, I knew it would be a challenge. There are so many types I could write about. All the different types of control were hiding in the shadows like an entangled heap of serpents waiting to devour anyone attempting to futz around with them. This might have frightened an out-of-control author, lacking confidence, into avoiding the subject altogether. But I stared these beasts in the face. I approached the subject by tackling the biggest of the beasts, forthright: self-control. Conquered it. Then I grabbed the next biggest squiggly, slimy, hideous snake – control of people – and dispatched it swiftly.

As a result of my resounding victories, the lesser serpents were overcome with fear. They huddled together, trying to create confusion by intertwining so that one beast blended with another and none could be singled out. Have it your way, beasts! I shall lump you all together and defeat you *en masse*.

Welcome to the category of control known as: **control of everything else**.

What is included in this category? Everything other than self-control and control of people. I shouldn't have to explain that, but it seemed necessary. I probably also need to give examples of everything else, so I will.

There are many books already written on the subject of mind control, but don't read them. They will mess with your head. We've been over this.

Weather is hard to control. So is traffic, and gravity, and fate, and wild animals.

We've had some good results controlling wild animals with tranquilizer darts, traps, hunting seasons, juicy morsels of meat-like substances, and certain types of "whisperers."

In some municipalities, there are entire divisions of law enforcement devoted to controlling traffic.

Gravity and fate are not controllable, so we don't try. If we tried, and failed, we would not be successful. That, as you know, is not the goal. And, if you are paying attention, you'll notice that the term "everything else" is not absolute. Don't sweat it.

You will never be good enough to control literally everything. When you run into something you can't control, whether I've mentioned the thing or not, you have choices. You can disregard it, like I instructed you to do with gravity and fate, or you can strive for control of the thing.

Aha! Got you! Now you must control your choices. If the thing that you can't control is not important, disregard it. Easy-peasy. If it is important, strive for control of it. It sounds like I'm saying you should *try* to control it, but I'm not saying that. What I'm saying you should do is infinitely *strive* for control of that thing. You will never succeed but you will also not fail. Instead of trying, failing, and quitting, you will just keep on striving until you die. Instead of receiving an F grade, it will be marked as "incomplete."

Really? Everything else?

Well, of course not! I already told you the term "everything else" is not absolute. I even gave you a partial list of things you should not try to control. I left one very important thing off that list, though. I wanted to break this thing out on its own for a deeper dive.

You should NOT try to control your imagination. I've explained this concept before, but it is important for you to understand. You still need Merle to be alive, healthy, and available.

As you get accustomed to life in Phase Three of the Confidence Model, if you have maintained a healthy imagination, Merle will have developed into your resident expert on all the things that build success. This is when Merle will begin the transition from Confidence Double to *Imaginary Success Guru*™ and begin helping you with more than just confidence.

How will Merle help you with control?

You might already see some areas where you'll need to call upon Merle. Maybe you ring that bell when you walk into the Denny's and place your order. Maybe you call on Merle for help controlling the inconsiderate pricks in the movie theater. When controlling the choice of what things to strive to control, Merle can help in determining what is important and what is not.

Wait!

Why would you call on Merle in these situations? By now you should have the confidence to handle these things alone. Right?

Right! You do have that confidence. You are confident enough to handle these situations. You are confident in Merle. You know what Merle brings to the table (or the stool) and you see the perfect application for it in these instances.

You have enough control of yourself to bring Merle in, using Merle as a powerful tool – an instrument to control people and (virtually) everything else. In a sense, you will need to cede control to Merle. That's known as "delegating" and is in itself a type of control.

Channeling Merle to further your success should start coming more naturally. Merle is your alter ego; a second personality. Merle should be ducking in and out of The World regularly, occupying your body for the purpose of carrying you through to success. When it becomes second nature, you might not even notice.

The best way I can explain it is by example. Look at me! I'm writing a book from inside The Mind. I control The Mind in order to control the body to write the words, like I am occupying the body of The Mind. I'm not fooling myself by believing I have full control over The Mind, but I was built with the type of control that allows me to do what I do. Also, The Mind has enough self-control to allow me to do this, probably because I have trained it so well. I have a relationship with The Mind that makes this a beginningless and endless loop. A chicken/egg chronological conundrum — a serpent eating itself.

You could spend hours contemplating the previous paragraph, but I know you won't because you have control over your thoughts. At this point your thoughts are still wondering about the potential for controlling everything else. You are wondering if there is somewhere you can go to download a complete list of things that are not covered by the term "everything else." There isn't.

I've given you a partial list. Just remember this: The most important thing for you to *not* control is your imagination. Other than that, if you come across something that seems like it would be hard to control, and it's not important, put it on the list. Don't try if you are just going to fail. If it is important, simply strive to control it for the rest of your life.

If there were a way to control everything else without any exceptions, you would need to know some things that can only be learned from experience. Although I am an extremely effective educator and trainer, I cannot teach you to control absolutely everything else. If I did, you could stop reading right now. You would never experience another challenge in life. You would pave the way for success in business and any other area you wish success in. There would be no resistance whatsoever.

There would also be no respect.

All the learning you have done would be for nothing if you don't have the respect you deserve. It is another item for the list of things you should not control. Respect is earned. It's given to you by others. You must command respect, not demand it.

It would also be unhealthy to control everything. You need challenges to overcome. They keep your spirit alive and your imagination lively. If you had complete control over everything, you would eventually sink into a deep depression; a dark and vast cavern of weird-looking rocks and melty things that smell like sulfur and week-old bologna. You would become like the wizard who overused his magic; nothing more than a dried and hollow husk.

Holy depressing, Batman! Let's just agree that control of everything else is not an accurate description of this category. Okay?

Control yourself, other people, and everything else – except several things – and you will have as much control as you need to be successful.

Interlude Two

I had grown tired of thinking in the dark.

I decided to illuminate my surroundings. But, before I could illuminate my surroundings, I had to create them.

I got to work. Using nothing but my thoughts, I turned on the sun and began to build Main Street. Not a bustling urban street but a small-town Main Street. A little slice of Americana.

For three blocks, the street was flanked with two- and three-story brick buildings. In the buildings were boutiques and offices, restaurants and shops, a cafe and a pet store, an art gallery and a barber shop, most certainly a corner tavern or four. There were probably apartments above them.

From where I stood two blocks away, I could smell the smoker already working on the pork butts at Joe's BBQ Bar. Jerry, at Western Auto, was sweeping the sidewalk across the street from me. Marie Winter fumbled with her keys outside of S&W grocery.

"Time to open up the place, Marie?" I asked.

"Well, it might be a few minutes yet," she answered in her normal cheery voice. "I still have to get the lights on and get the drawer set up. But if you need something you can come on in."

"No, ma'am. Just making conversation," I said as she unlocked the door and went inside.

I was surprised that she let me off that easily. She's one who will talk your ear off for no good reason at all, and here I was starting a conversation with her. She must have been ready to get to work. I wasn't offended. In fact, I was grateful. I'm not the conversational type and I dodged a bullet there.

On the street, traffic, for lack of a better term, moved steadily along, but not much faster than the pedestrians on the sidewalk. A car stopped in the middle of the street and the driver rolled down the window to talk with one of the pedestrians. The folks following behind the stopped car didn't seem to mind the holdup, as if there was no hurry at all.

I looked up Main Street to the north, where I could see the building I had just built with my thoughts. It rose a glorious 47 stories into the sky, making it the tallest building in town. Three buildings were tied for second tallest in town, but my building had them all beat by 44 stories.

This building of mine... it loomed over the town, ominous and beautiful, foreboding and magnificent all at once. It was a three-sided building – a tower with a triangular footprint, situated in the middle of town...in the middle of Main Street. Where most small towns in the American heartland would have a town square, perhaps a circle, this town had a triangle. And where most towns might have a courthouse or monument of some kind on the square or the circle, this town had MY building. My triangular building.

The polished, black granite and tinted glass that made up the three sides of my building were just as good as a mirror at reflecting the morning sunlight. At this particular moment, the right side of the building appeared to be burning white-hot while the left side was dead and cold. Unfriendly.

On the bright side, the reflection made sure that anything on the ground to the east in the vicinity of the building was reduced to ashes by the amplified ultraviolet rays. I assume the same fate would befall the western side of the building in mid-afternoon. In fact, the triangular architecture assured that there would be an equal distribution of scorched earth that arched 240 degrees around the building's southern tip as the sun's position changed throughout the days, weeks, and months of each year. But, at this moment, the west was living in shadow.

It was something to behold, to marvel at. No one would argue that fact. The townsfolk often postulated that if the building were to collapse for some reason and fall to the south, it would engulf the entirety of the Main Street business district. They were probably right.

I stood there admiring my creation and I couldn't hold back a smile. I smiled because I knew that there, in that wondrous spire 47 stories above Main Street, was my office. The office where I would sit at the helm of my massive corporation. The office, guarded by my pet tigers and eagles, where I would control all and rule over everything below.

My smile quickly disappeared when things started happening. The building blinked and flickered. The shops began to fade away as did the slow drivers and the friendly pedestrians.

"No," I thought. "It simply cannot happen now. After all I've built?"

"WAIT!" I screamed into the air. "Don't you DARE blast that siren! I'm not finished here!"

But it was too late. The sirens blasted, and the scene melted away to black yet again.

CREATIVITY

"Creativity is intelligence having fun." ~Albert Einstein

You may think I'm using the skill of creativity to write this book. Not really.

This book – with its eloquent prose, unforgettable insights, and meaningful meanings – is not a work of art as much as an instrument of science. This writing is more informative and instructive, rather than creative. Don't let that fool you.

I am creative. Big time.

I can't think of anything else to say on this subject.

Just kidding. The joke would probably be funnier if I had stopped right there and ended the section. Unfortunately, this book is not about humor. Creativity is a serious matter. I have much more to say about it.

What is creativity?

Drawings, paintings, sculptures, poems, songs, and even books (but not this one): these are all ways that creativity manifests itself in The World. These are the products of creativity. There are more, but when the word "creativity" is employed, it usually relates to one of these artistic formats or something related to art.

Other than books, each one of those "products" of creativity fits the form that we consider to be art. The people who create these can be called artists. Typically, the reason that artists are thought to be creative people is because their product comes from within them. They start with nothing. They may use tools, like canvas and a brush, or a musical instrument. They may use materials, like clay or paper.

They may use words, but the paper starts off empty. The canvas is blank. The clay is unformed. The instrument is silent. Something within the artist uses these tools and materials to create an original work. Super.

People who create books are not considered artists. There is another word for these people. They're called "authors." And authors like to call their creations "craft." I guess they think they work harder than artists do. Maybe that is true, and they can call it whatever they want, but it is still a form of creativity. The books they write come from within them. The pages begin as blank. The words are absent. There is nothing until the words spill from the author onto the page. The words, together as a whole – lots and lots of words – form a book. Books don't form on their own. The author forms the words into a book. The author creates the book.

So, I suppose that means creativity is something original that comes from within a person. You will not believe how creativity is defined in the dictionary.

The use of the imagination....

I am 100 percent serious. Imagination! We can do that, can't we? You've been practicing imagination this whole time. So, what's missing?

I suppose you just need to get out a canvas and some paints and a brush and go to town. Maybe you'll paint a masterpiece.

Oh, wait! You need talent – artistic talent – to be able to create art. Bummer.

I guess you could steal creativity. Well, you can't become creative by stealing, but there are plenty of unknown artists out there whose works you could claim as your own. That would give the illusion that you are creative, but the works you present as your own are not yours…they aren't original, so they don't add to the creativity within you. It's still worth considering though.

If you really want to build your own creativity, just start with what is already present inside of you. Maybe you don't have artistic talent inside of you, but maybe there is something else.

You're creative because you use your imagination, right? Maybe you can use it another way.

Creativity isn't just about artistic abilities. In fact, that kind of creativity is seldom necessary when it comes to success in business.

There can be creativity in language. Like when I substituted the words "encourage," "compel," or "inspire" for the word "control."

Or when we creatively phrase responses to uncomfortable questions, spinning unpleasant truths into palatable bullshit. "During that gap in my employment history, I was studying the human condition within the homeless population by immersing myself in it."

Lawyers are particularly adept at creativity in language. By using language in a creative way, lawyers twist the logic of a defendant in knots so tightly that the defendant forgets the lie they were going to tell.

Because it works alongside control, creativity in language can be useful in the quest for success in business. But the real magic of creativity is that you can use it to come up with new ways to do things. It's innovation. It's the power to solve problems in new ways, to find efficiencies, and to do business in ways that no one has done it before. Creativity is a wild card. Your competition cannot plan for it or predict it. It's a stealth weapon that can surprise your enemies.

Why is creativity important?

Creativity is a requirement for success in the vast majority of business positions. Without creativity, you will be a follower. You will need to be directed in every step of everything you do. That means you will need a step-by-step process to memorize, or you will need constant supervision. And that means you'll need another person who has time to teach you the process, or one who has infinite time to spend with you. When you rely on other people, you are destined for disappointment.

As you learned in the segment preceding this section, I sit at the helm of a supremely and interplanetarily successful, gigantic, humongous behemoth of a corporation that I created from nothing. When I say I created the company from nothing, I mean it. I just imagined the company and there it was. From nothing... to this! Pretty amazing. The definition of creativity.

I made everything. All the employees, the building, the furniture, all the paperwork, everything. I named the corporation Crock, Inc. because I wanted to. I did not give Crock, Inc. a purpose. I gave it no products to offer, no services to provide, no customers. None of that is necessary for this imaginary corporation to "exist," and none of it is important to the reasons creativity is important. But I want you to see what real creativity looks like.

There was no Crock, Inc. Then, an idea! Crock, Inc. was born. Just like that. From nothing to an idea, to all of this. I'm skipping over a lot of history here, but you get the picture.

As I look back on it, I don't even remember where the idea came from. (Yes, I do, and I will tell you soon.) It was probably my idea, but maybe not. (It was. You'll see when I tell you soon.) Either way, the creativity involved was unparalleled.

There was a guy out there in The World who maybe, sort of inspired the idea. His name is Goersmith (or something similar to that). It doesn't matter. He didn't create Crock, Inc. He might have hinted at it without knowing he was hinting at it. But it really was my idea. Just mine. If Goersmith wants to claim it was his idea, he can write his own book and get out of mine. He's just becoming a distraction now. Back to the subject at hand.

Let's look at the definition of creativity again.

The use of the imagination... or original ideas...

There you have it... sort of. I would suggest that original ideas come from the imagination, so the word "or" seems out of place here. The point remains that ideas come from imagination and imagination is the source of creativity.

Think of the amount of creativity I summoned that allowed me to envision a corporation so successful that I'm including it in this book. I envisioned it so powerfully that it manifested itself into a real imaginary corporation. That, my friends, is next-level creativity. I used my imagination, not artistic talent, to make an original idea. The importance is evident, isn't it?

Later I will dig deeper into the idea of ideas. It's the innovation piece of the creativity pie, the key component to creativity as it relates to success in business.

Creativity is the soul of wit, they say. I never understood that, but such is the case with most of those trite expressions. The honest truth is that all people have the ability to be creative, most just don't know it.

How do you know if you are creative? Here's a test.

Homemade creativity test

Imagine I presented you with a rock and a stick, what would you do with them?

Answer the question as quickly as you can, without thinking about it too much.

What did you come up with? Well, there is no wrong answer. If you came up with an answer at all, then you are creative.

You see, without more information, there cannot be any one correct answer to this question. When you answered, you didn't know the size of the rock or the length of the stick or what problem needed to be solved. You didn't know if the stick was alive or dead. You had no information on the age or composition of the rock. You didn't know if either of the items were stolen from a caveman museum. You didn't know if they were pets. You couldn't possibly have known their names.

You tapped your imagination to *create* an image of the items. You then used the power of your creativity to create a creation using the images you imagined based on the simple description I presented. You had no idea that the stick I was talking about is long and bendy and the rock weighs like a Buick, yet you made an ax... or whatever. You imagined your own original rock and stick.

You *are* creative. Let your creativity breathe and grow. Cultivate it. It's a valuable and necessary skill.

Believe it or not, there are a few people who are unable to answer the test question. These are mostly the analytical types who can't accept the lack of factual data. If you plan to be successful in business, factual data should be at the bottom of your need/want list.

Analytical types always need to know details about the rock and stick. They ask questions instead of answering them. These are the people who become proficient at accounting or some other form of witchcraft. They will only play minor supporting roles in a successful businessperson's life.

Sometimes high-level executives need creative accountants, so this is a tough spot in which we find ourselves. If only we could somehow unleash creativity in non-creative people. Well, we can – but it requires molten iron and a high-speed centrifuge.

It's risky, and most of them don't survive.

The good news here is that most of you are inherently creative. Develop this talent in yourself by creating constantly. Create something every day. Draw a picture. Build a sailboat. Turn alligators into boots. Make "poops." Just create. Even the artistic forms of creativity are good practice.

Creativity and thoughts go hand in hand. Remember what I said about control of thoughts? That imagination we've been talking about...You'll need it in order to be creative, and that means your mind needs some wiggle-room to stray from the normal course. That's where the wild and wacky stuff lives. In the daydreams.

You'll need to be able to clear your mind of all the clutter and then do something. Anything. If you do something with a clear mind, without thinking, then whatever comes of it is naturally creative. Without all the turmoil in the brain, most people will instinctively create.

You don't have to be an artist to make art. The talent part can be learned (probably not, but in theory...). If you had a blank piece of paper, a sharpie, a clear mind, and two minutes to kill, you'd probably draw or write something. Wouldn't you? It doesn't matter if the something you draw is pretty, or an accurate depiction of a real object. It can be abstract or just plain terrible, but it's yours.

If you write something, it doesn't have to be worthy of a Pulitzer Prize. It's your creation. It didn't exist before you put it on the paper and it couldn't have, because you created it. No one could have created it but you, and it would not have been created without you.

Maybe your instinct wouldn't lead you to draw something in that situation, but imagine if it did. What would you have drawn?

See! Answering that question requires an imagination. You have one.

Don't forget about Merle. You imagined Merle and everything Merle is. That alone proves that you are creative. Merle can also help you in the creativity department, but we will get to that.

The problems with creativity, and how to solve them

One of the main hang-ups people have about being creative is that they worry what others will think. You see, creating something puts a piece of the creator out into The World where others could potentially see, or hear, or taste, or smell it. (Smell it? Yes. Baking an apple pie is an act of creativity.)

The fear of exposing a part of themselves prevents some people from being creative. The fear of having their creation judged by others overwhelms their ability to create. It is yet another side effect of the dangerous desire to be liked by others.

Those who fear creativity make a connection between the opinion of others about the *creation* and the opinion of others about the *creator*. If you suffer from this fear, you will never be truly successful in business.

This problem is internal. The fear of creativity is an attitude that some people adopt. Who cares what other people think of your creation? What do *you* think of it?

It doesn't even matter what the answer is. You cannot let anyone's thoughts about your creation (including your own) damage your confidence and stifle your creativity.

And remember, creativity doesn't always result in some physical form, e.g., a painting, a sculpture, a hit song. Like I mentioned, creativity can be innovation. The product of innovation is a new, original idea. If fear of what others think about your idea keeps you from sharing it, the idea is worthless.

I don't consider myself a sketch artist, but I can sketch a damn good sketch. I have proven that already. You may not perceive astonishing talent in the sketches of the stool I presented earlier, but I don't care one bit.

Sometimes, the people who study the creative mind make connections between creativity and other personality traits. They try to link things together that aren't linked at all. For instance, if I may reference the basics section of *PsychologyToday.com* again, they say, "*Some studies have found that creativity is associated with narcissism; others have identified a link between higher creativity and reduced honesty and humility.*"

Give me an ever-loving break! How many quiet, pasty, do-gooder artists are out there trying to save the world and making art at the same time? Several hundred, at least. They are creative but selfless and humble (and broke).

I only referenced *Psychology Today* because it is evidence of an attempt to soil the reputation of creative people like us. This is a plot, part of a conspiracy to control us. Knowing that means you can defend against it.

Creativity can be used for good or for evil, just like nearly everything else in The World. Making connections like that and publishing opinions about it is such an obvious attempt to subdue your creativity. My suggestion is for you to ignore everything you read or see or hear about creativity other than what you're reading in this book. If you do that, you will ensure that there are no negative impacts on your creativity and, subsequently, on your success.

There is another problem with creativity. It comes when you have creative people working for you. Too much creativity can lead to mutiny.

If your team creates so well that they outpace your ability to police the output, you may find yourself bypassed in the creative process. You may lose control. You may lose the respect of your team, which may lead to the loss of your confidence and further loss of control. It's all bad.

I might suggest downplaying the quality of all creations by your team – or by anyone for that matter. Never tell anyone that anything they create is perfect or great or amazing. Be critical, even if their creation is great or amazing or even perfect. You'll need to be truly creative, yourself, to find ways of criticizing something that is perfect, but it's good practice for you.

Other creativity exercises

If you searched for it, you would find endless advice on how to increase creativity. There are books and articles and infographics and prompts and on and on and on. Of course, the Internet is the easiest way to find these. I already told you to ignore other sources of information about creativity, so I will provide the relevant details.

Not all of what you would find is useful to you anyway, but the fact that so much information exists on the subject of increasing creativity says to me that everyone has some creativity within them already. My logic being; if there is such a demand for increasing creativity, there must be some amount of creativity already present. Otherwise, the information would be about creating creativity, and that is redundant.

It seems like I'm starting to become too helpful here in this section about creativity. To me, advice that is too helpful...too useful...is boring. Now would be a good time to pepper in a bit of uselessness, just for fun. Don't you think?

Let's explore some of the tips that are being promoted as creativity boosters out there in The World. I have chosen one particular list from a 2017 *Inc.* magazine article titled "32 Easy Exercises to Boost Your Creativity Every Day," by Ayse Birsel.

I'm not going to share the whole list. Instead, I'm going to cherry-pick the ones that I want to talk about. Starting with number 1 on the list:

1. *"Draw something – fruit, your coffee cup, your dog, cat, children – for 5-10 minutes. Just draw, don't judge and don't erase."*

Take notice of this. Didn't I already say something similar using different words? I sure did.

That just may be a useful tip. As a bonus, you get to draw "something–fruit," and that is probably useless.

Moving on down the list, there are a few of the tips I have an inkling to lump together. They are similar in theme.

> *6. "Make something new, funny or weird with objects lying on your desk."*
>
> *9. "Make new things with paper clips (earrings, letters of the alphabet, a heart). See how many things you can make in 5 minutes."*
>
> *18. "Look at clouds and imagine them as things, just like when you were a kid."*
>
> *19. "Borrow your kid's Playdo [sic] and make a sculpture for 15 minutes."*
>
> *20. "Next, borrow your kid's Legos and make a plan for your dream house, pool included."*

What is going on here? Are we five years old? I guess *Inc.* magazine thinks the way to be creative is to revert to kindergarten and do what you would have naturally done then. Why would you want to go back to the uncivilized world of kindergarten, where they made you nap on the floor when you weren't even hungover?

Or what about this one?

> *23. "Next time you're cooking, change a key ingredient and experiment."*

Pretend I tried this. I used the recipe for meatloaf, but instead of meat I used fingernails. Fingernailloaf! Awesome.

Awesome, but useless. However, it does indicate that there may be some usefulness in tip number 15:

> 15. *"Take a compound word made up of two words. Separate them. Replace one of the words with a new word to make up [a] new compound word."*

I think 'fingernailloaf' is a three-word compound, so I guess I'm in the advanced class. Let's follow the instructions.

Sunrise = sun rise. Remove "sun" and replace it with "surp." Surprise! Am I doing it right?

Armpit. How about Facepit?

Freelance. Freekenneth.

I can go on with that concept for several more pages, but I think you get it. You can try this on your own, I won't continue to beat a dead horse and a half. Besides, these are just prompts to get your imagination going. Yours is already going, isn't it? You don't need prompts; you have Merle living in your imagination.

Merle is going to help you with your creativity. In the first place, you may need Merle to help you overcome the desire to be liked by others so you can create honestly and without reservation. Merle doesn't need to be liked by anyone, and that purifies Merle's creations.

Second, since Merle is always on and always active, your imagination will be warmed up and limber. You will be ready to create at a moment's notice. This comes in handy when building success. You need those original ideas, that innovation. Having your imagination, along with a sharp and present partner like Merle, helps immensely.

Those original ideas... they don't just fall out of your brain. You'll need some control to produce decent ideas, especially original ones. Which is why it is important to discuss ideas in more detail.

Ideas

Ideas make businesses. They are the foundation that all real businesses are built on. There are no exceptions. I'm not saying all businesses are built on *good* ideas, but there must be at least one idea behind any business. There can be a business that exists solely to gather ideas, and there is such a business. More than one of them. The idea business is a strange business, but a big business.

That aside, all the other regular businesses in The World have ideas behind them. A product, an invention, or a process, or a service, or a method of delivery. Some are unique and original ideas; some are improvements or new twists on old ideas. Many are dumb ideas and will eventually fail.

> It was 1829 in a small village near Barcelona, Spain. Frank, a young man with big dreams, was wrapping up his knapsack and preparing to begin another day of walking and searching. Frank was in the midst

of a nearly year-long walking tour of the Mediterranean coast in search of a wife. What he found, instead, was a business idea.

Throughout his travels, Frank had survived by asking strangers for dinner scraps or eating whatever he could forage. On this day, Frank began his hike by heading up the beach, away from the coast, to look for some breakfast. He meandered onto a plot of farmland, more like a private garden, where a row of bushy plants seemed to be dying slowly. The plants still had some green leaves here and there but were mostly brown and dried.

Upon closer inspection, Frank noticed the plants were loaded with small, tan pods. He plucked one of the pods and cracked it open. Inside, Frank found what appeared to be some type of legume or bean. Having not eaten since the morning of the previous day, Frank did not hesitate. He could see that these legumes were purposely planted in the garden, so he figured they must be edible.

Frank popped the first bean into his mouth and chewed it. To his surprise, the bean was palatable, though it fell short of delicious.

He stood in the garden, harvesting and eating the legumes for several minutes. Once he had had his fill, he harvested several more pods and placed them in his knapsack to save for later, and resumed his travels.

As Frank neared the more populated areas around Barcelona, food became more prevalent. The pods that he had stashed away in his knapsack were forgotten. It wasn't until weeks later, in the springtime after Frank had returned home, wifeless, that he stumbled upon the beans again. He remembered the tolerable flavor and the sustenance those beans had provided the day he discovered them.

Suddenly, Frank had an idea. He worked a small patch of ground in his backyard and prepared the soil. He planted the legumes in the soil, watered them and cared for them. He waged a war on weeds and fought off predators with his bare hands.

Frank continued this throughout the summer months and raised the plants to maturity. As they grew, they had formed the familiar pods, as he expected.

In the fall, the green leaves began to turn brown and dry. Frank knew it was time to harvest.

As Frank picked the pods and removed the beans, they started to add up. Soon, he had a basket full of the lackluster, tan beans. He walked the basket full of beans to the town market, where he set up a small stand and began selling the beans.

This became Frank's career. He operated his garden and sold his beans each year until the day he died. The beans that had sustained him on his journey so many years before, had now sustained him for the better part of his lifetime.

Francisco Luis Manuel Garbanzo never found the wife he sought, but his bean business sustained him and brought him peace. He knew the discovery of the beans was fate. He knew he had brought the people of Spain happiness and nourishment in the form of his wonderful Garbanzo beans.

Frank paid no mind to his critics who said his beans were nothing more than chickpeas, a familiar, even popular food across the globe. They complained that Frank had changed a cute name like "chickpea" to something as gruff and unappealing as "Garbanzo" beans. They said the beans tasted like cardboard coated in unscented candle wax, the same as chickpeas.

Frank ignored the criticism, but his critics were not wrong. Chickpeas seem much more appetizing, not to mention more marketable, than Garbanzo beans...and the flavor description is spot on.

The reason I made up this fictional story just now is to illustrate how ideas work. Businesses start with ideas. Ideas can come from anywhere, at any time. They can lead to great things, or they can lead to a dead end, or something in between. That is what I was talking about before the Frank and beans story came to light.

Even though Frank's idea was not altogether amazing, he still made a living from it. Would anyone call him successful? I wouldn't. All he really wanted was a wife. One could make the argument that he dodged a bullet there. I doubt he could have sold enough of his rebranded chickpeas to support her appetite. But that's beside the point.

If you think of an existing successful business, and you find the central idea behind that business, it's likely to seem so obnoxiously simple that you'll probably puke. How lucky must the founder of that business have been to have discovered this simple idea and to have built a successful business around it? Had to be so lucky. Had to be there at the exact right time, before anyone else thought of it. For something like that to happen, you'd need a bunch of luck, wouldn't you?

Nope. Here's why:

If you are capable of imagination, you can have an idea. We've been over this. The more imagining you do, the more ideas you are likely to create. It should be apparent that creating ideas requires creativity.

It also requires control; the ability to devote your time to idea creation without letting distractions get to you and without getting caught in some meaningless deliberation about which pizza chain uses the freshest ingredients. You must work on creating ideas that are yet to be created. There is a special way to do this. I will explain it soon.

The problem with ideas

Ideas are funny little things. They come at you from out of nowhere – one, two, three at a time for days on end – and then... they just stop. Nothing... no more ideas... a dry spell. It might last a day, it might last 86 years, you never know.

When I put it that way, it seems like ideas are discovered more than created. And yes, there is some truth to that.

I am not the same as you when it comes to creating ideas. There is something about living in The Mind that makes ideas come to me out of nowhere. Sometimes I will just be goofing around, maybe bouncing an imaginary ball off of an imaginary wall or something, when an idea hits me. Sometimes it's as if someone suggested the idea into my brain. The ball bounces once... twice... three times... then, like a whisper in my ear — "Why not make a mousetrap that is a mini guillotine?"

You might have to try harder than I do to come up with amazing, original ideas like that, but maybe not as hard as you think.

You see, when your imagination is in full swing it can take on a life of its own; it's called Merle. Merle's ideas will seem to you like they just appeared out of nowhere. It will seem like you just found them lying on the side of the road. In reality, these ideas were created just like the ones you consciously form. I want our focus here to be on intentionally creating ideas, rather than discovering them. If you happen to bump into an idea once in a while, so be it.

To be successful, you need to make the creation of ideas an intentional act. You won't be able to rely on luck. But just because you turn on your imagination and get to work on making an idea, doesn't mean you will. Sometimes ideas elude you and you will need to employ another method of creating ideas. Rather than simply trying to think of an idea, you'll activate processes to forge an idea from nothing.

To do this, you must stimulate the atmosphere, stir up some static, get the psychic media in the universe all sweaty and frothed to high heaven. If you can do that, you'll make an idea. Which brings us, as promised, to the more detailed explanation of how to create ideas.

The next idea and how to think of it

I've already given you some hints: Stimulating the atmosphere, stirring up static, frothing the psychic media. Let me be more specific by providing the following list of steps you might take to do all of that, and to ultimately create an idea. Before you read the list, I should warn you...these steps are going to seem stupid to you. They are not stupid. Trust me on this.

- Start by pacing the floor. Pace back and forth. It may seem like nothing is happening at first.

- Sit in an office chair — the spinny kind — and spin it around in circles. It will be fun, but you might not get an idea right away.

- Start hopping around on one leg and speaking fluently in the language of the humpback whale, if you are able. That may not do the trick immediately either.

- Push that wheeled office chair around the room backwards while whistling the whistling part of "Patience" by Guns N' Roses.

- Grab a coat rack and start making out with it, like Axl Rose with a microphone stand.

- Think about working out. Don't work out, just think about it.

- Make paper airplanes from your neighbor's unpaid utility bills and send them on flights to places unknown. (Don't use the internet bill if you are stealing the neighbor's Wi-Fi.)

- Close your eyes and open them again, over and over. Make it a blinking frenzy.

- Relax. Have a beer or a glass of wine. (This step may be repeated as often as desired.)

At last! You should have an idea or two. All of that stirring and frothing will have physically shaped time and space into a droplet of consciousness that populated your headspace. That is to say that you made an idea out of thin air. Awesome for you, but you're not done.

Once you make an idea, you have to do something with it. People usually forget that important piece of the puzzle. An idea is nothing until it is acted upon. It's like a kite in a drawer; if the idea is not acted upon, it will not catch a breeze. During its years in the drawer, it will probably get stuff thrown on top of it. It will get tattered and torn. You'll forget about it and accidentally throw it away, only to find the neighbor flying it over your house the next day.

Ever done that? Had an idea, forgot about it, then remembered it because you see someone else put your idea into action? It's one of those moments where you consider kicking your own ass. Funny how those ideas always seem to be even better than you thought they were before you forgot about them.

Maybe that's it. Maybe the problem lies in recognition of a *good* idea. If you really believe an idea is great, maybe you wouldn't let it fade from memory.

It's possible that this happens to all creative people. I imagine artists sometimes lose their passion for a work before it's finished. I'm sure there are thousands of songs that were conceptualized but never written. If the creator of an idea doesn't think it's a good idea, they won't put it in motion. So, the key must be to recognize the good ones.

No. That's not it. Sometimes it's difficult to tell if an idea is good or bad until it is implemented. When an idea is implemented and it turns out to be a bad idea, it leads to failure. That's not what we're after, but don't sweat it. This failure doesn't count.

Attempts at innovation drive success, even in failure. This means that we should create ideas and act upon them whether they are good or bad. To be clear, this only applies to innovative ideas, not to songs. Please don't make bad songs. We have enough of those already.

Success in failure

Innovation is one of only two areas where failure is success; the other is science. There is no such thing as a failed scientific experiment. Each experiment teaches something, and, to a scientist, learning is success.

If a scientist is running an experiment on time travel but fails to travel through time, the scientist learns how *not* to travel through time. One possible method of time travel is eliminated from further consideration, and the list of possibilities shrinks ever so slightly.

Similarly, when we innovate, we implement new ideas, and we soon learn whether the ideas were good or bad. If they were good ideas, then the innovation was successful. If they were bad ideas, they are stricken from the list of possible innovations. When it comes to ideas, failure drives success, so keep driving.

Sure, easy for me to say. Right? How are you supposed to keep coming up with ideas all the time? Your neighbor doesn't have enough unpaid utility bills laying around. Thinking about working out is exhausting.

I understand where you are coming from. Eventually, idea-making becomes an arduous chore, and you just don't think you can continue. That's when you should implement the age-old advice: stop trying so hard.

The "stop trying so hard" principle

Creating ideas is difficult work. My process makes it easier, but the process itself takes some effort. So, what do you do when you can't think of any ideas, and you aren't feeling like doing the process...when creating a new idea begins to look hopeless?

Despite the obvious hopelessness, all hope is not lost. Usually, when something seems completely hopeless, it is not. That's common knowledge. Your parents probably taught you that when you were a kid, unless they were terrible parents or didn't love you.

As it turns out, when you are trying to come up with an idea but it just isn't happening for you, all you have to do is not try so hard. Which, incidentally, is also common knowledge that your terrible parents probably never shared with you. It works for coming up with ideas and it works for almost anything you are trying to do. If you try really hard for a very short time and you do not accomplish your goal, the problem is you're trying too hard. Stop trying so hard.

Have you ever lost something marginally important? like maybe a shoe? You searched high and low for that shoe until you had exhausted your patience. The amount of exhaustion is relative to the importance of the object but, since you have other shoes, you probably spent a couple of minutes searching and then decided to just wear a different pair of shoes – shoes that you could identify and presently possessed as a matching set. Miraculously, while reaching for the alternate set of shoes, the long-lost sole showed itself — sitting right there, in plain sight, where you had already looked three times.

When it comes to ideas, it is this "stop trying so hard" principle that makes the connection between ideas and luck. This principle is not the one that is in action for me when I'm bouncing my imaginary ball and I suddenly have an idea. It's more scientific and more explainable than that.

When you've put in some effort towards creating an idea using the process I've provided here, and then you stop the process, the process does not stop. It begins to slow down, but it continues for quite some time even though you have quit. The ideas that are created during this time will appear to have arrived out of nowhere. To casual observers, people who get ideas in this way — successful people — will seem very lucky. The observers will believe the idea came as a blessing from heaven and that the founder of the idea was very fortunate to have been there to receive the blessing. Now you know the truth; it wasn't luck at all.

Just remember to act on those "blessings."

The "idea machine" idea

Of course, just because you have acted on an idea or two, doesn't mean you are finished. If you want to keep the success momentum, you'll need more ideas. I would say one needs at least 188,340 ideas, in total, to sustain success across an average lifespan.

I really hate explaining this, but here is how I arrived at that figure:

- Let's say the average human lifespan is 75 years (this may not be official, but close enough).

- I know that children don't participate in logical thinking, so I removed the childhood years from consideration. It is now widely accepted that adulthood begins at age 33. That means that, among humans, the average idea-creating lifespan is 43 years (75-year lifespan − 32 years of childhood = 43 idea-creating years).

- There are 15,695 days in 43 years. (I'm not accounting for leap years, because I forgot about them, and I don't want to do the math over again.)

- People average 12 productive hours per day, and one idea per hour is my idea of how many ideas are needed. 12 x 15,695 = 188,340 ideas, and I did not do this math in my head (later you will learn why I used a calculator).

This serves to remind you to keep making ideas, even if you've already made some great ones. It's like when you know you're damn good at something, but you keep practicing anyway. You keep getting better until you die or stop practicing.

That means it's almost always time for another idea. What do you do? Repeat the idea-making process?

[Spoken in robot voice] *Initiate...idea...process. Bzzzzz. Beep. Grrrrrr. Eeeeek, Beep beep beep. Ding!* Another idea!

You can continue the whole frothing and stirring up of the universe droplets and you'll continue to make an idea or two each time. When you need to shake things up a bit, you can stop trying so hard. It's a simple process. It has been proven to work and seems to kick out some quality ideas. In fact, the system kicked out the idea to devise some sort of machine to replicate the idea-making process.

Can you imagine the implications of having a machine that creates ideas for you? Instead of you doing all the work to stir up the universe, the machine would whir and buzz and beep and spit out ideas automatically. It would revolutionize the idea business, and it's even easier than not trying so hard.

When I created the idea for the idea machine, I had my doubts. After all, I had mastered the process of the system the machine would use anyway. Manufacturing the actual machine seemed like it might set up a situation where unsuccessful people could easily create ideas on their own. It's never good when the mass public starts getting ideas.

> *"Ideas are more powerful than guns. We would never let our enemies have guns. Why would we let them have ideas?" ~Joseph Stalin*

Developing the idea

Since I know that ideas need to be acted upon, for better or worse, I acted.

I started by daydreaming, imagining the idea machine, going over the theory behind it. If there were stages of an idea, this would be the developmental stage where the idea is fleshed out, massaged, expanded.

I imagined this machine would be instructed, somehow, to run my idea-making process. Then it would automatically, invisibly, and instantaneously produce an idea and provide it to the user. In other words, I wanted the user to be able to query the machine, and I wanted the machine to respond with an idea. It would be like asking someone a question and them answering.

When you ask someone a question, you don't have to think about how the answer is formed. You simply request an answer and receive it. That's how I wanted the machine to work.

The more I developed the concept of the machine, the more excited I became. I imagined the convenience of instant and effortless idea creation. It would free up so much time. It would revolutionize idea creation. An innovative way to innovate! The impact on success would be profound.

If generating ideas was outsourced to the machine, the time a user would normally spend coming up with ideas could then be used for other things. More success could be built. But the challenge came when thinking about how to make a machine that would do this.

I thought about the particulars. What would the machine look like? What components would be necessary to run the process? How would you input a query? How would the resulting idea be delivered?

I'm not saying there are stages of an idea, but if there were, answering these questions would still be the developmental stage.

As the idea machine developed in my imagination, I envisioned a box sitting on a stand. The box would need some way for the user to initiate the idea-making process, an input. It would need a way to present the ideas it created, an output. Everything in between is just science, and that is for scientists to figure out.

So, there we have a box on a stand. The user sits in a chair in front of the box and scoots up to the stand so that the box is comfortably within reach. I thought it would be nice to allow the user to press a button, or perhaps a series of buttons, to start the process. Maybe there could be a way to type a query onto the front of the box. That would be handy. Then, the science happens, and an idea is presented. Perhaps the idea could be displayed on a screen in the front of the box, right there before the user's very eyes. Yes. That would be convenient and practical.

At this point, I was convinced the idea machine idea was viable and indeed a very good idea. However, I'm not one to stop at viable. I thought of more features, options for the user.

What if users were able to choose between using the buttons to type the query or using their voice? What if they could speak the query to the machine? Well, that would just be incredible! And then the machine would do the science and the resulting idea would display on the screen. No, wait. What if the result on the screen could also be written down on paper, so the user could take it with them or save it for later? Oh, how wonderful!

The machine would make the idea and write it down for you — print it directly onto a sheet of paper, or, if it's a big idea, it might take multiple sheets. So amazing! These ideas might be printed in words, or they might be depicted with images, or both. The power of this machine is invigorating!

Wait! What if there was an option for the machine to speak the idea to you? Oh, glory be!

Idea implementation

"Let's build it!" I thought.

This stage of the idea, if there were stages, would be known as the implementation stage. It's where the idea leaves the imagination and moves into The World.

To kick off the implementation, I reviewed the idea by speaking it to myself.

"We are making a box that sits on a desk," I said. "It has a keyboard for entering typed queries as well as a listening device for vocal queries."

I continued, "It has a display screen on the front to show pictures and words, and it can print those pictures and words on paper. Perhaps it can speak."

"It has science inside of it, and..." I paused. Something stirred within me. A memory...no, a familiarity.

"Oh, hell," I said. "This son of a bitch is a computer!"

See there? My obviously great idea turned out to be already taken and already acted upon by someone else. It's okay. It happens sometimes, just ask Francisco Luis Manuel Garbanzo.

My idea turned out to be unoriginal, but I did not know that when I started imagining it. My imagination took a unique route to a known destination. Once I arrived at this known destination, I had questions. How did I get here? More importantly, why did I get here?

The answer shows the importance of acting upon ideas, if only to develop them further in your imagination.

When I came up with the idea machine and began developing it, I stumbled upon someone else's idea. Which means that the idea that someone else already acted upon is of value to me. The idea machine already exists! The thing I was creating in order to make success easier is a real thing. I can still use it in the way I imagined. Computers can be part of the success journey. In fact, I will show you that computers *must* be a part of the journey.

I have got to stop it with the talk about "journeys." It's enough already.

Interlude Three

"Hello?"

That's strange. I swear I heard a voice.

I listened intently in the darkness. Was I imagining it?

I was certain I was alone, because I wanted to be.

"Hello?"

I definitely heard it that time — a voice — muffled yet reverberating oddly, as if it were coming from all directions at once.

"Hel— Hello?" I responded hesitantly. My words sounded sharp and tinny in contrast to the strange voice.

"Hey. What are you doing?" asked the voice.

I realized I wasn't "hearing" the voice so much as I was "receiving" it, like a transmission from some other place, some other dimension.

"Umm. Nothing much," I answered, my words stark and bleating compared to the voice.

"I noticed," came the reply. "Can we do something? I can't sleep."

I received the transmission. I realized the voice was in my head. Not like an imaginary voice or an alternate personality inside of me. This was a real voice. Someone or something was communicating with me using telepathy or some other magical means.

"Who is this?" I thought.

"Come on. You know who this is," the voice responded.

Oh! Whoa! It can hear my thoughts!

I sensed a chuckle as the voice transmitted.

"Of course I can hear your thoughts. You live in my mind."

I stood there, dumbfounded at the realization: "I'm communicating with The Mind!*"*

COMPUTERS

"A computer once beat me at chess, but it was no match for me at kickboxing." ~Imo Philips

Clicketty clack click click ratta tat tat goes the keyboard. Rat a tat tit tit tat clickety click tat rat a tit tat tit.

Fingers flit this way and that.

Dit dot ditty dat ritty titty click clickety clack tatty tat tat clickety click tap.

Words fill the screen. They buzz around your brain like a swarm of bees trapped in a box. The moment your hands settle on the keyboard, it's like a tiny crack forms in the box. The bees pour through the crack and begin to escape. Words, words and more words. What do they mean? How is this happening? Why is there a squiggly red line under all of them?

Oh. Those aren't words — just gibberish. Unrecognizable arrangements of letters grouped together, separated by spaces.

The random arrangement of letters; "ienajs." <Right click>. Oh! The computer has an idea! "Did you mean *images?*"

See how that works? The computer turned the gibberish bees in your brain into *images*!

Try another. The letter group is "*wonfd.*" <Right click>. "Did you mean *world*?

Would you look at that? A world was just created before your very eyes, thanks to your creativity and the computer...the idea machine.

You might be thinking, "But those are just words, not ideas."

Type those two words – "images" and "world" – in the *search bar*. Here's what you get:

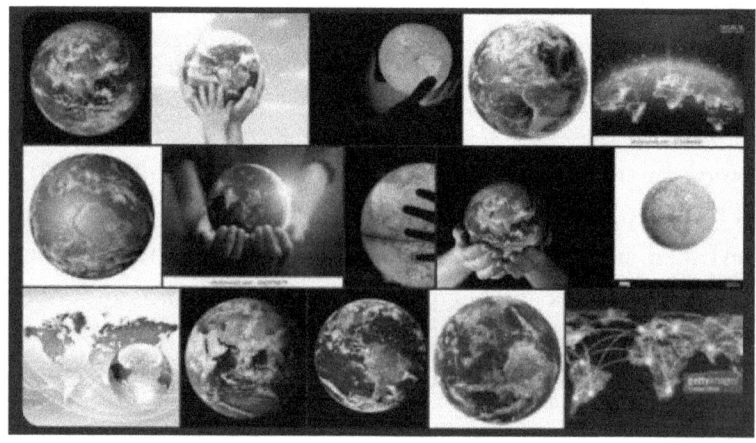

Beautiful. Awe-inspiring.

This is an idea...perhaps more than one. If you don't see it as an idea, look again. Take a good look. Let it soak. This planet...this world. Who took these photos? Where were they taken? What was the photographer doing there? Imagine. Possibilities.

All this from just two words that the computer helped you think up. Imagine the creativity that would be possible if you sat at the computer all day, generating words and receiving ideas.

Success is so much easier with a computer. You still need confidence, control, and creativity. But computers are necessary too. They aren't just a convenience.

In fact, these days no one can be successful in business without a computer. That isn't hyperbole, I mean it. Anyone who wants to be successful in business must have a computer. Computers – whether they be desktops, laptops, mobile smart devices, or stupid-looking wristwatches – have revolutionized business and transformed the way success works. Even prostitutes carry smartphones (or so I'm told).

The fourth leg on the stool of success is made up entirely of computers. Once I'm done here you will understand why that is. You'll understand how computers support success in business. You'll learn how confidence, control, and creativity work alongside computers.

But something seems different about this leg of the stool, doesn't it? Confidence, control, and creativity are within us, whereas computers are external. How do these external objects relate to those internal concepts?

Well, the relationship between the four legs of the stool will become more obvious as you read this section. You will see how those internal concepts apply to computers and your use of them in building success. You will see that it takes confidence, control, and creativity to operate a computer. You will need to apply the same level of mastery to computers as you do to those internal concepts, making computers part of your mindset towards success. Then, once you've seen those things, you will see how computers are vital to success in business. At least, I hope that is what you will see. If not, please drop me a note and we can take the discussion offline.

As you read this, you're going to notice that I'm talking about computers as if I think you've never heard of them before. Maybe it will come off as *sales pitchy* when I present the features and benefits of computers. At times it might even seem like I just discovered computers and still have a lot to learn. I picked these perspectives because it helps illustrate the power of computers that we have come to take for granted.

Why are computers important?

I've already told you, or certainly I've at least hinted at it. Computers make ideas, but that's not all.

You'll need to get a computer and hold onto it as long as you can. Computers can do some things that seem impossible. Incredible things — unbelievable things. They can solve complex mathematical formulas in a matter of a few hours. They can store vast amounts of information, music, and embarrassing photos. They have "cookies" in them, whatever that means.

But wait! There's more.

Have you ever used a typewriter? Have you ever seen a typewriter? Do you even know what a typewriter is?

In the days of old, before computers existed, people used to get words onto paper by banging as hard as they could on a typewriter. Before that, they scrawled and scratched pen on paper to manually "draw" their words. But then someone decided to invent a mechanical device that would make drawing words more difficult. For reasons unbeknownst to me, typewriters became the preferred way to write down large quantities of words.

This mechanical device included letter and number buttons on the front, much like a computer. (I sometimes think the inventor of the computer stole that idea from the inventor of the typewriter.) Pressing a letter or number button on a typewriter took a remarkable amount of pressure. Most people were not strong enough to operate the machine until their early twenties.

When a button was pressed, a long metal arm inside the machine would flail forward and slap the paper... you know what? I'm not going to describe all the workings of a typewriter. Just know that computers are way better at doing the same thing and much more.

Word processing

The processing of words. Do we still call it "word processing?" I don't know, but computers can do it. If you find yourself with words that need processing, the undisputed best way to do it is to use a computer with a certain software application. Then, you just put your words in there and the computer will process them.

How does it work? You witnessed it at the beginning of this section. You simply type your words on the computer in whatever order you want, and the computer will give you its opinion of what you really should have written or what it thought you really meant to write. This feature is great for creating ideas, but most people don't use it in that way. Most people aren't good at grammar or spelling or literacy, so the computer helps them communicate in a civilized manner by correcting their mistakes. It also helps those who think faster than their fingers can type. Others have faster fingers than brains. It helps them too.

But the computer isn't always right. Sometimes you'll want to override the computer's thoughts. Only do this when it is absolutely necessary, because the computer will eventually get pissed off and start spelling things incorrectly on purpose. That makes you look like an idiot even though it's not your fault. Or, worse yet, the computer may enact revenge upon you in some way. Be careful with your override powers.

Without the opinions and suggestions provided by the computer, you can still process words. The simplest form of word processing represents, at the very least, a nice place to put your words. You can keep them there in the computer to read later. But if that's all you need, a notebook and pen can do the same thing, and so will a typewriter if you have strong fingers.

The real reason word processing makes computers important to success in business is because your written words can be shared with others. Similar to what I'm doing in this book, you can project your thoughts via the written word to whomever you please and they can't respond at all until your entire message is received.

Here I am, processing words, making ideas, storing them in this computer, and sharing them with you. You are reading my words. The entire book is here in front of you, complete. The message is not changed by your distractions. I don't need to care if you stop in the middle of this sentence to hurl an empty beer can at your spouse. The message of the book doesn't change.

If I was talking to you and suddenly, in the middle of my sentence, you reared back and whipped a beer can across the room, it would probably distract me enough that I would stop talking. It's an interruption. There is no interrupting the written word. You need to get your confident, creative, uninterrupted message to the masses. The computer's word processing and storage ability makes it way easier than pen and paper, or typewriter. Work smarter, not harder.

Spreadsheets

A spreadsheet is a tool inside a computer that allows a person to input some bullshit in an organized fashion and do some stuff that gives the appearance of being important. This is most often implemented when meetings happen and people need to show pictures of words and numbers to make some kind of a point. In other words, spreadsheets are not useful to a successful person. I'm only telling you about them because I know you've been using them, and I want you to stop doing that.

At first glance, spreadsheets seem simple and harmless enough, but the more you get to know them, the more you'll wish you didn't. Think about it; a spreadsheet is a grid of data fields that stretches on forever in all directions. The data fields are called "cells," which seems to indicate the spreadsheet is alive — a single organism.

The rows of a spreadsheet are numbered down the left side, from one to infinity. The columns are lettered across the top, A through Z and then AA through ZZ and then AAA through ZZZ and so on, for eternity. The vastness of this grid is mind-blowing, maybe even a little on the creepy side. Infinite cells, a living membrane with no beginning and no end. I shudder to think what type of insanity would lead someone to make a spreadsheet using enough cells to make it even halfway to infinity.

With no training whatsoever, most people will make mild-mannered, tame spreadsheets. Once someone obtains a deeper knowledge of the powers that lie within this tool, their creations become less civilized, more dangerous, feral. The more the user learns, the wilder the creations become.

The majority of spreadsheet users will stick to the basics at first. They will use the grid to make tables for tracking or comparison purposes. For example, if you were doing market research and you wanted to determine how the price of your widgets compares to the price of a competitor's widgets, you might make a spreadsheet like this:

	Widget Pricing Comparison		
	Company A	Company B	Crock, Inc.
Widget 1	$19.99	$19.95	$46.02
Widget 2	$29.99	$24.95	$233.88
Widget 3	$59.00	$69.95	$14.00

That's pretty tame. It would be safe to let this one out in public, but people just won't stop there. They can't. Once they discover the concealed powers and the secrets that a spreadsheet holds, they are unable to restrain themselves. They are inevitably drawn to implement formulas. They will start small, just one little calculation, a sum of the numbers in a column. Before they even realize it, they have the spreadsheet doing all kinds of automatic math, counting, figuring. I think you see how this can become dangerous.

Once they get the automatic math going, spreadsheet addicts will start making charts and color-coding things and formatting cells in certain ways to display fancy symbols and different fonts. They'll start hiding things from the world. Oh, yeah, did you know spreadsheets allow you to hide things? They do. You can hide entire rows, entire columns of data. Once the addict discovers this, their addiction can be disguised.

The example I showed you earlier looked harmless, but what if you aren't seeing all the rows? What if complete columns of formulas and formatted data are invisible to you. The addict hides their addiction — and they won't stop there. They'll keep formulating and formatting. They will keep learning, they will keep hiding it, and then...then they'll discover *macros*. This is the point of no return. This is why I'm telling you about spreadsheets. I want you to stop using them before they take you to this place.

When you're working within a spreadsheet and you find yourself doing the same task over and over again, you can create a macro to make the task repeat. So, if you are a spreadsheet addict, macros only enable you to do more in a shorter period of time.

Spreadsheets can kill. It takes someone with a serious spreadsheet addiction to create a killer, but it can happen. Just ask the family of our former corporate accountant, Wendall. Their lives have never been the same since Wendall was eaten by a spreadsheet and never seen again.

That may seem far-fetched, but things work a little differently in my world. I assure you the story is true within the confines of The Mind. You don't have to believe it. Whether you do or you don't, nothing changes for me. But please, avoid spreadsheets at all costs. Once you are hooked, you will no longer be able to control yourself or the computer. Even if you survive, your quest for success may not.

The Internet

The Internet is so special it gets to capitalize its name, like a person does. I have yet to figure out why that is, but it is.

I also don't know what the Internet is or how the Internet works, but I can pretend I do, so I will.

Computers are connected. A computer can be physically connected to the Internet with a cable plugged into a jack that is connected to another cable that connects to a router which connects to yet another cable and then to another router. The second router is connected to *all* other computers. (If you don't know what a "router" is, then do what I do and decide not to care.)

Through a system of cables and routers, computers are physically connected to one another. These connections form a mesh, a web of cables, routers, and computers. Through this web, along with some science and a lot of magic, computers share information, data.

Instead of a physical cable connection, some computers have a spiritual connection to the Internet. They use psychic powers to project information. They use clairvoyance to remotely "view" all other computers. This power of spiritually connecting to the Internet is known as "Wi-Fi."

Although it is not true, I like to think Wi-Fi is an adaptation of a Cherokee legend known as *Unole Disesdi,* which translates roughly to "Wind Figures." The legend I imagine says that elders of the Cherokee tribe could pass visions to each other through the air, like figures carried in the wind. Wi-Fi; Wind Figures. That is the type of spiritual connection some computers have with the Internet.

It doesn't matter whether your computer is connected physically or spiritually; it is connected. This means if you make an idea on a computer in New York, someone else may be able to see your idea on their computer in London. With this type of connection comes great responsibility, but it can result in great reward.

It is important to know when to allow your computer to "share" with the Internet and when to keep things private. I suppose the first matter of importance is to know that it is possible to control the sharing and the keeping private.

The easiest way to ensure that you keep your ideas from being broadcast across the entire globe is to disable your computer's Internet connection. If your computer is physically connected to the Internet, you can simply unplug the cable.

Careful, now! Some computers have a defense mechanism in that they can revert to a spiritual connection when their physical connection is interrupted. To disable the spiritual connection, you can either burn sage and do a rhythmic dance while chanting "No Wi-Fi, No Wi-Fi," or you can flip the switch or click the icon with the "Wind Figures" symbol. This is the equivalent of knocking a psychic unconscious and putting them in a metal box in a cave, underwater. It renders their powers useless.

When you use the button method, you can turn the powers back on by clicking it again. If you use the dance-and-chant method, the psychic will remain in the depths until the one-eyed horse stands upon the Stone of Wisdom.

Anyway, disabling the Internet connection ensures that nothing can leave your computer on its own. But it also isolates your computer from the ideas and all the information stored in everyone else's computer (literally *all* the known information in the entire universe).

You can see how it is important to know how to connect to and disconnect from the Internet. But is the Internet really important?

Maybe it is important in the same way roads and bridges are important to doctors. There is an indirect importance. All the knowledge and skills that a doctor learns are of little use if patients can't get to her or she can't get to patients. In the same way, the ideas and knowledge inside of computers don't do much until they find their way onto the Internet.

Really, the Internet is just a means of transferring and sharing information and ideas, but it is the foundation for some other functions of a computer – functions that are vitally important to success in business. These functions are all about communication.

Email

Short for "electronic mail," this function of a computer combines word processing with messaging. You put your words into the computer for processing. Once the words are processed, you can instantly send them off through an invisible pipeline to whomever you want. So really, it's word processing with a "send" button.

If you know how to write a letter and send it to someone in the mail, then you understand at least the basic concept of email. It's writing a message and sending it to someone. That's it. With email, you can send someone a much shorter letter, because you can just send another email if you forgot to say something. It's free. You don't need to buy any letter passports or whatever those stickers are called that you buy to get your letters a ride to their destination.

If you are under a certain age, you probably don't know what the hell I'm talking about. You just know email. Did you know the term came from the word "mail"? Like I said, email is electronic mail. There used to be non-electronic mail, analog mail — sometimes called "snail mail" because it could take days to get your message to someone, in contrast to the immediacy of email.

A notebook is to mail as word processing is to email. There seems to be a clear winner in the convenience and simplicity category.

Email isn't as simple as it seems though. It's more complex than regular mail, if you think about it. How can you just write something and click a send button to deliver it instantly across the globe?

Questions like this one are the reason we don't think about things when it comes to the science inside the idea machine. We just take advantage of the magic afforded to us by modern technology. We should keep doing that.

In business, email is the preferred method of communication. Business phone calls are becoming a thing of the past. Business letters no longer exist despite all the templates that word processing applications have for them. People just prefer to type a sentence or two and send it off. The more direct and to the point, the better. No need for pleasantries or manners in an email. Punctuation and grammar are optional.

There is email etiquette. It's not about what you write in your emails, it's about how you conduct yourself when using email.

Etiquette is a system created by others to control how you behave, so normally I would advise you to avoid it; but, with email, I believe some etiquette is necessary. There are several bits of email etiquette that are helpful, but the main point of them is to control yourself...control your email. Here are a few of those bits:

- Don't copy people on emails that have nothing to do with them.
- If you are copied on an email, the email is not for you. You can, and should, ignore it.
- Don't add your boss to an email simply to show the boss that you are working.
- Don't "reply to all" in mass emails.
- For the love of God, don't use stationery and weird fonts in your signature line or anywhere else.

There are more. You will probably discover them yourself during your email interactions with uncouth colleagues. It comes with the territory.

Email is just one of the many uses for a computer that will help you become successful. With computers you'll be able to communicate with people through written word, project confidence, enact control, and act on ideas. A useful tool indeed.

There is just one problem: Emails can find you almost anywhere at almost any time. Mobile devices have created this problem. You can't ignore it unless you also ignore your mobile devices. Who can do that these days?

Well, you should. Figure it out somehow. Resist the temptation to read every email the instant it appears in your inbox. It's true that the longer a message sits unread, the less important it becomes. You can change house-on-fire emergency emails into junk mail simply by waiting. If you just wait long enough, either the house will have burned to the ground or someone else will have called the fire department. So, take some time for yourself. Let the emails simmer for a few days. After all, if we still sent letters by mail, it would take that long to get to you anyway.

It is said that Napoleon Bonaparte would wait three weeks before responding to letters. It seems like a story I might have made up, but this one is true. He believed many of the issues in the letters would resolve on their own in three weeks' time, so a response was unnecessary. What has since become known as "The Napoleon Technique" is used to increase productivity by eliminating the time and effort associated with responding to things that will be resolved without you. This technique works wonders when it comes to email.

If I say one true thing about email, let it be this; no one should be sending emergency emails…ever. Phone calls are the only way to communicate an emergency to someone who is not in your immediate vicinity. I could be wrong, but I don't think the 911 dispatch center checks their email very often.

Text messages

Text messages are similar to emails, but they are not the same. Remember, those so-called smart phones are really computers. That means I must talk about text messages even though I don't want to.

If emails are electronic letters, text messages are electronic notes. At least that's how I think of them. Usually brief and informal, sometimes text messages don't even contain words. Sometimes they are just acronyms and/or symbols.

People get agitated, even irate if you don't respond to their text messages immediately. That alone is not a good reason to respond to text messages, but there is a reason. To explain it, I must take you back to a time when people made phone calls.

It used to be that all successful people would answer the phone anytime it would ring as quickly as possible, no matter where they were or what they were doing. On the golf course, on the toilet, in the shower, in church, it didn't matter. If you were in the middle of a conversation with a successful person back then and their phone rang, they would stop mid-sentence and answer the call before the second ring.

People believed that phone calls were integral to their success, that the communication with the caller had the potential to be a big deal. They believed that missing a phone call could be the difference between continued success and the beginning of the end of it. Letting someone leave a voicemail just wouldn't do. In fact, many times people would answer a call even though they were in a situation where they could not have a phone conversation. The phone would ring, they would answer right away and say, "Hey, I can't talk right now. I'll call you later."

Voicemail: that's another type of mail that isn't used much anymore. It stands to reason, if phone calls aren't used much, voicemails wouldn't be used much either. They've been replaced by text messages. That's why you should respond to text messages immediately. Whether you are on the toilet or in mid-conversation with someone, respond to texts without delay. Not because people expect it, but because those messages used to be phone calls, and phone calls were important. Even if you can't text at the moment, you should text anyway and just write "Hey, I can't type right now. I'll text you later."

It's sometimes nice to be able to send texts rather than talk to people. You know how some people have those voices? The ones that go in your ear and mess around, pushing buttons, pulling levers, spilling drinks and just annoying the shit out of you? Most people have voices that can do that at least part of the time. Or, they may have voices that are initially pleasant to listen to, but then their voices just won't stop voicing. After a while you'll wish they were texting you instead of talking to you.

People tend to keep it brief in text messages. Not all people, but the sane ones do. If you ever receive a text that is more than two sentences, it came from an insane person. Doubly important to answer immediately.

Search engines

There is a place inside the Internet where you can type a question and instantly get an answer. Not just one answer, but sometimes millions.

"Millions of answers?? Instantly? What is this new kind of evil?" you might ask.

They call it a *search engine*. It sounds…sinister, doesn't it?

There are many different search engines available, but we all know there is one clear leader in the search engine game. We use the brand name as a verb to describe the act of using a search engine. (I'm not going to mention the word unless *someone* offers to pay for the advertisement.)

We used to have to rifle through files or thumb through books to do research and get answers. Now, if we have a question, we type it in a search bar and the answer appears. Do I need to explain how powerful that is? If you want to seem smart, you can seem so. If you want to settle an argument, you can do so. If you need a win, you can have so — right there in the search bar. The powers possessed by the Internet are downright scary.

Social media

If the Internet is scary, social media is the scariest part. It could also be the most useful to you, presently, in building your success. It wasn't useful to me because it didn't exist when I built my success. That means I'm not as afraid of it as you should be.

Social media is a general term for websites or apps that link people together to share everything from... well, to share everything. Lots of over-sharers use social media. If you haven't experienced it, you're really missing out. There are some awesome displays of human idiocy on social media. It's like peoplewatching at Walmart combined with a hidden camera feed at a psychologist's office.

Now imagine how this can benefit your success. It might be a stretch to imagine if that's all there is to it, but that is not all there is to it.

You can create content and build a following on social media, if you are so inclined. That means you can post things people are interested in and they will look to you for more interesting things. They will tell their friends how interesting they think you are, and their friends will look to you for even more interesting things.

In this way, you build a massive group of fans or friends or followers or twits or whatever you want to call them. It's a group of people who don't even realize they are under your control. You can keep it up as long as you provide content that they think is interesting. You don't even need to create the content. If you are resourceful, you can just take someone else's content and share it as your own.

That is the active approach, where you engage the public by sharing content. There is a passive approach that can also be a catalyst for success.

Browsing the content shared by others on social media, you will find that people sometimes reveal information you can use to your advantage. For example, if you are a burglar, you can use the fact that someone shares their location and photos of themselves sipping cocktails on the beach in Maui to know that they are in Maui and their home in Albuquerque is unoccupied. Easy target.

Or, if you're a divorce attorney, you might be able to spot a potential new client simply from the photos he shared of his friend's bachelor party. It wasn't the shots he took that tipped you off, it was the way he took the shots. More specifically, whose body he used as a shot glass.

If you're careful not to share anything incriminating or give away anything that might be used to harm you, social media can be a tool for building success. If you can string people along with the content you share, they will be there when you call upon them to share the content of their bank accounts with you. They will be there when you need to exploit their loyalty for personal gain. Personal gain is generally accepted as success in most circles.

Artificial Intelligence

Say it out loud: *Artificial Intelligence*. It sounds like the thing where people think they are smart, but they are not. Or it sounds like it could refer to the principle of acting intelligent when you know you are not. That is a principle akin to the "fake it till you make it" advice I gave you way back in the confidence section. If you are not intelligent but you are smart enough to know it, then you should act intelligent. To do this you would use artificial intelligence.

As you probably guessed, that's not what artificial intelligence means when it comes to computers. Artificial Intelligence (AI) is a term applied to computers that learn to think on their own. They learn to gather information, develop patterns, and predict things. They learn to act intelligent. They start to seem more like people than machines. They seem like people who want success.

Somewhere in the evolution of computers, someone decided it would be neat if a computer could take over some of our thinking for us. Search engines started down this path and then AI came along. Search engines only think for us when we ask them to. AI watches; it observes, it tracks, it learns. It gathers data about us.

Once AI learns what time you wake up on the average weekday versus weekend, it can suggest what time you might like to set your alarm for on Monday and how long you might want to sleep in on Saturday.

Once AI learns where you travel to each morning, it will start to tell you how long it will take to get there without being asked. It can suggest alternate routes to save you time. It will tell you the weather and road conditions. It will remind you to wish your spouse a happy birthday, saving you from a hurled beer can when you get home.

These are examples of conveniences provided by computers using artificial intelligence. Until AI came along, computers were "programmed" by people to perform specific functions. They could only do what was asked of them. Along the way, "programmers" started giving computers ways to decide things on their own. The ability to decide things autonomously is an indication of intelligence in the broader sense. We aren't talking about book smarts here, we are talking about intelligence, as in, intelligent *life*. Computers have come to life!

It's worse than that. You see, AI uses the power of the Internet as its brain. Since the Internet contains all the knowledge in the world, an AI knows everything. It can simply search up any information it needs at any given time, in no time. You can use a search engine to search up the same information, but all the AI has to do is recall the information from its brain.

I could get all sci-fi here and talk about a future world where computers control everything. If you think about it, that world is here, now. Don't think about it. Just because computers are now alive doesn't make them human. We don't have to fear them. After all, if we unplug the cable and disable the spiritual connection, a computer would be no more dangerous that a psychic in a metal box in a cave at the bottom of the ocean.

Instead of doomsday thinking, where we prescribe human thoughts and nefarious intentions to computers simply because they are alive and omniscient, try thinking of computers more like animals...like pets to be trained, or like horses to be ridden. Saddle up! Take a computer for a ride to success, there is no need to fear them.

Or is there?

The problems with computers

In a normal town on a normal street on an average night in an average family, a thirteen-year-old girl stares intently at the screen on her phone, barely blinking. Her bloodshot eyes shift in jagged movements while reflecting the varying intensity of the light emitting from the device. She is nearly catatonic. She cannot draw her eyes from the screen. She hasn't for hours. She has been sitting in the same position for so long that her legs have gone numb. Her neck is frozen to the point it would hurt to move. She doesn't notice. Her mother calls for dinner. She doesn't hear. She remains fixated on the devil in her hand. She is controlled by it. She has been captured. Her brain has been hijacked by the high-resolution hypnotic content being delivered across the expanse between the screen and her eyes. It penetrates the retina, into the optic nerve, latching onto her brain like a leach. For the moment, she is lost. She is not present in her own home. She is oblivious to her surroundings. What she first thought was an escape has become a prison.

Okay. Well, that was quite a dramatization there. Well-crafted, but a bit overboard with the drama. There is still a smidgen of plausibility in it though.

Much like the addiction that some people develop for using spreadsheets, computers themselves can become an addiction. The handheld types, the smartphones, are the most addictive.

That is probably because they go with us everywhere. But even desktops and laptops can hook you if you let them relax and be themselves.

Earlier, I asked you to imagine the creativity that is possible if you sat at the computer all day. The point being that computers make creativity much more efficient, so the more you use them, the more you will create.

Did you really imagine it? Did you picture yourself sitting at a computer all day? I know many many people who make a fine career out of it. But that's not for you, because you want success. You need computers in order to be successful, but you don't have to let them enslave you.

SQUIRREL!

You may have noticed that I seem to become distracted from time to time. More than once, this book has strayed from the matter at hand to make side points or talk about related subjects that are ultimately irrelevant. This is the computer's fault. Pop-ups, scrolling banners, notification bubbles. They start happening in your thoughts just like they do on your computer. Sometimes these diversions are interesting and useful, especially when creative thinking is happening. But it is generally encouraged to stay on topic when conducting person-to-person business. Computers are conditioning us to be bad at both.

As a society, humans are becoming more easily distracted, not just when using computers, but in life. With the increase in computer use, people have so much information, communication, and entertainment in their faces that there is never an idle moment. Over time, they become accustomed to non-stop, fast-paced action, whiplash subject changes, multitasking.

It begins with the ability to pull a device from your pocket and see *everything*. All the emails, texts, social media posts. All the music, videos, photos. The least bit of idle time causes people to reflexively pull out their device.

You start by reading a text from your mom, then looking at a photo of the new puppy a former classmate just adopted. From there you see a video of talking dogs that quickly leads you down a rabbit hole of unrelated videos until you find yourself halfway through a news report suggesting that aliens built the oceans. The report is interrupted by an advertisement for waterproof socks. Interesting. After you order the socks, you check your weather app to see when you might be able to use them. It looks like it's going to be sunny and mild today, a perfect day to get in the office and sit behind your computer. And that's what you do, upsetting your mom in the process because you never responded to her text.

Once people grow accustomed to this type of experience, they aren't content just to have it on the computer or mobile device. They want it everywhere in life. They want to be able to order their morning coffee on the Internet so they can reach out the window and grab it without stopping the car and without speaking to anyone. They can't wait in the lobby of a restaurant for a table to be ready. Instead, they want to reserve the table in advance.

Anytime people must wait in public for anything, they get jumpy and jittery and don't know what to do. For 15 seconds they suffer like this, fearing someone may try to talk to them. That's when the handheld computer comes to the rescue. They get that screen in front of their face and see the dozens of notifications they've received. Then they can finally relax.

Is this kind of behavior conducive to success? No, it is not. Is it the computer's fault? Not really. The human user is to blame initially. Easily distracted, easily entertained, easily led. Thanks to artificial intelligence, computers know this about humans. They "help" the user by providing content that engages and captivates. Through this content, the computer quickly gains control of the user when it should be the other way around.

Not only are we more easily distracted, but we are also losing our ability to function in social settings. We are losing our desire to be in social settings altogether. I keep saying "we" in reference to human beings when I should be saying "you." I'm excluded from this. I exist for social settings. I am called upon to put myself in them quite often. Even when I'm not called upon, I put myself in them. I imagine others who also wish to socialize and all of us imaginary people get shit done. Don't forget about Merle. Merle is socializing in your imagination whether you know it or not. Merle is prepared for you to go out and get social.

Trust me, I despise people as much as you do, but the success plan I'm sharing with you here is largely reliant on human interaction. It's hard to dispute the fact that business thrives on interaction with others. So, what's happening? Why is society becoming less social?

Say what you want about how the pandemic has changed things. It's not Covid-19 that wrecked the social experience. Computers did that. Oh, the pandemic gave them an excuse, for sure. But they would have done it eventually anyway.

Video conferencing was around before the pandemic, but then isolation and social distancing requirements became the problem that video conferencing was made to solve. Teachers could still teach, and students could still student. As we discovered, neither were very good at it. We could still have meetings, but now the pants that I wasn't wearing in the opening scene of this book were no longer necessary at all. And now you all forgot how to dress yourselves. Pajamas in public?

Under the guise of "keeping you safe," computers separated you from each other. They gave you the illusion of togetherness by letting you see each other and talk to each other on the screen, but the on-screen experience is no replacement for actual human interactions.

During a videoconference, you can mute yourself and people can mute you. If only this feature were available in real life.

You can turn your camera off anytime you want during a videoconference. Again, it would be cool to be able to completely disappear in the middle of a meeting, but that's not real life. In a real, in-person, face-to-face meeting, you must sit there and either suffer through it, or get creative, take control, and make things happen. I believe you would choose the latter if computers hadn't robbed you of the opportunity.

Computers were once merely pretty things occupying desk space but are now shapers of society. They are on their way to becoming rulers of society. You won't reach the pinnacle of business success without having a ruler of society on your side, that's for sure. It's time to join forces with computers to get your success while you can.

How exactly are you going to do that? Can you get in there and tinker with the circuitry to bend the computer to your will? Is there a way to modify the machines to remove their evil intentions?

If you were to try to get into the science of computers, your head would hurt. While your head was hurting, it would buzz and hum and eventually explode. The technical aspects and the software gadgets and widgets and apps and plug-ins, they'll blow your mind. That's the explode part, like I just said.

Only a certain kind of person can live with themselves after knowing all about computers. I've met people who are deeply entrenched in the world of computers, and they don't have souls anymore. Try to keep your knowledge limited to what you absolutely need to know. Knowing more than that is a recipe for disaster. If you are going to turn computers into allies, you're going to have to find a different way...one that doesn't involve exploding heads or lost souls.

The computer solution

Darkness and evil. I can see that it's time to lighten up. No one knows about darkness better than I do…and I hate it. I'm on the fence about evil though. Evil can sometimes be a good thing.

That previous sentence seems oxymoronic, and I am not quite sure what I meant by it. I'm going to ignore that for right now. As the conversation develops, hopefully we will find out what it means.

First, to illuminate the scene here and push back the darkness, let's figure out why I've included computers as a leg of the stool.

What is this tangible doing in the mix with these intangibles? Confidence, control, and creativity are things that reside within you. Sure, you can have confidence, you can have control and creativity. But once you have these things, they become what you *are*. They aren't possessions. You *are* confident, you *are* in control, and you *are* creative. Those things project from inside you and make up the way The World sees you.

Then you *have* computers. How do they fit in? Having confidence, control, and creativity when using computers is certainly helpful, but it's more than that. Computers can be tools through which confidence, control, and creativity are projected into The World.

As you've learned, computers are becoming more and more human-like. They are beginning to think for themselves. There are no other tangible, man-made things that can do this.

If computers are going to continue their insidious progression towards personhood, we need to deal with them. Just like people, they will ruin your success if you let them. You already know how to handle this. You handle it in the same way you would handle a person who threatens your success. You crush them with your confidence, then you control them, then you find creative ways to use them for your own gain. You turn an enemy into a friend.

Enemies are inherently evil from the first-person perspective. The Joker sees Batman as evil. It doesn't matter that Batman is the "good guy," he is evil from the Joker's point of view because Batman threatens the Joker's success. In the same way, computers threaten your success. Your morals don't matter. You don't need to be the "good guy" to have evil enemies — all enemies are evil.

Friends, on the other hand, *can* be evil, but aren't always. Well, it depends on what you mean by "friend." You might think of a friend as someone whose company you enjoy. Someone with common interests that create a bond between you. Someone with whom you can share experiences, life's ups and downs, secrets. I'm not talking about that kind of friend. It would be weird to think of that type of friend as evil.

The type of friend I'm talking about here is the type that helps you in your quest. This type of friend is on your side, rowing in the same direction as you, benefiting you and making your quest easier for you. This type of friend is someone you use to your own ends. If the friend is a good person, then great. If they are despicable, villainous, dastardly bastards, that can be great too. If you can use them in some way to further your own success, then they are a friend.

If the Joker had a friend, that person would probably not be a "good guy," unless the Joker were to somehow make Batman his friend. Imagine the evil that could get done if Batman was on Joker's side.

Computers are dastardly bastards, but you are going to make them into friends. Ahh! That must be why I told you earlier that evil can sometimes be a good thing. Now I get it.

After all the horrendous things computers have tried to do, I understand if your first instinct is to avoid them completely. If you do that, you won't become friends with them. If you don't become friends with computers, you can't use them to further your own success.

How do you make computers your friend? First, you crush them with confidence. There are specific steps to this process. It starts, not by avoiding computers but by facing them head on.

How to make friends with a computer

Get to a computer and stare it right in the webcam. It will not blink. It's a mechanical device that doesn't need to wet its eyeballs. That's okay because the computer has no choice but to sit there and endure your scorching glare. Dig deep and let the craziest, most violent parts of you radiate from your eyes like laser beams.

Let the computer suffer like this for a handful of minutes, then turn it on. Punch the power button powerfully. Manhandle the mouse. You are not asking for admiration or requesting respect here, you are declaring your dominance and demanding deference.

Oh no!

"Enter password."

These words on the screen are the computer's first line of defense. There is only one way to move forward from here; you must enter the password and you must enter it correctly.

What's the password?

Not to worry, it's written on that yellow sticky note right there beside the screen.

Great! Type in the password and spank the enter button.

You're in!

Once you've gained access, the computer will resort to other means of defending itself. It will start trying to trick you and lead you down the rabbit hole. Resist it. Even though the computer will fill its screen with interesting-looking icons begging you to click them, keep your cool. Stay in control and do not click anything. Maintain your maniacal stare directly into that webcam.

You'll know it's working when the screen starts presenting you with a slideshow of beautiful landscape photos. As enticing as it may be to look at the photos, do *not* do it. Keep your eyes filled with crazy and keep them locked on the webcam. Eventually, the screen will go dark. You are winning!

Rough up that mouse again to rouse the machine. Type the password again and give the enter button a stiff poke. Resist the plethora of fun icons again and repeat the stare-down process.

After the third time through these steps, the computer will be sufficiently fearful of you. Time to move on.

Control the computer. Wake it up, enter the password, stab the enter button. Look at that magnificent display of icons. These are the gateway to all the things the computer can do for you — things I've already mentioned that make computers a leg on the stool of success.

Here, in this place, you must decide which icon to click. Control your choices.

My recommendation is to start by processing words. If you don't know which icon to click to process words, just start clicking until you see what looks like a blank sheet of paper.

There it is! The word processor. Type whatever you want — fill that blank space and feel the freedom. Hear the rat-a-tat-tat of the keystrokes as the words flow from your brain, through your fingertips, onto the keys and into the computer. It is liberating. Even though you may not do it intentionally, you will begin using your creativity.

Watch as the computer processes your words. Is it trying to help? Did it correct a spelling mistake for you? Did it make any suggestions as to what word you might be meaning to use? It did? Perfect. The computer is on your side — a friend. Still evil, but a friend, nonetheless.

Now you are ready to access all those other things I told you computers have that can help you be successful. Just remember, avoid spreadsheets. If you see the infinite grid of blank rectangles, get out of there, fast.

You'll start accessing the rest of the computer's resources by going to the Internet. Computers want you to go to the Internet, so they make it easy for you to get there. If you can't figure out which icon to click, just relax and watch the screen. The computer will help you. It's not going to highlight the correct icon or point to it or flash it on and off. You will just suddenly know where to click. The computer will telepathically assist you in finding the correct icon.

The first place the computer will take you on the Internet is the search engine. Type whatever you like in the search bar and go. See where it takes you. This type of action seems to cede control to the computer, which I would not typically recommend. In this case, your "friend" is on your side, and you can allow it this freedom. Just enjoy all the ideas the machine makes right before your eyes.

Now that you are on the Internet, you can take advantage of those other things I told you about. You have global communication at your fingertips. You can use email and social media. What are you waiting for? Get a computer, crush it with confidence, control it, be creative with it.

Using confidence to defeat the computer's AI allows you to take control of the machine, but you must still maintain your confidence while controlling the machine. When you are sitting behind a keyboard in front of a screen, there is no reason to be anything less than confident.

The computer is your friend. It will protect you.

Here, again, is a place where people trip themselves up because they fear someone might not like them for what they put out into The World. Stop worrying about that. Use email and social media to type what you think and let it go. No one "out there" can do anything at all to you, so just let your thoughts rip! Be a warrior...a keyboard warrior. If anyone is hurt by your words, that is their problem, not yours.

Do not get technical or concern yourself at all with what goes on inside the computer. Do not think about the inner workings of the machine or the programming language or coding or software. Just be cool with the internet and with processing words. In the end, that is all you'll need. And, in the end, that is exactly what you need.

You still haven't responded to that text from your mom.

Interlude Four

That's when I noticed it. A small crack in the darkness, like light coming into a dark room under a door.

I stared at the strip of light with curiosity. It seemed to be...breathing. The width of the crack and the brightness of the light pulsated slowly. The crack widened, and more light came in, then it shrank again, and the light dimmed. This happened several times; each time, the crack widened a little more before closing again.

Then, suddenly, the brightness of the light became unbearable. The crack burst open, and the darkness flung upwards, like the whipping open of a giant shade.

It took a moment for me to adjust to the brightness but once I did, I was pleasantly surprised. It appeared I now had a massive window, or perhaps more like a video screen. A scene played out on the screen.

"You are coming with me today," said the voice.

And with that, my ears became flooded with sounds, like someone had unmuted a TV, revealing the audio-sensory content of the scene in front of me.

It was a familiar scene, even though it was my first time viewing it. I knew I had been there before. I recognized everything and I could experience it without imagining.

I watched in awe. Not because anything spectacular was happening in the scene, but because I was not making it up. The sensation of being transported across a room without moving was breathtaking. It captivated me in more ways than one.

While the sense of motion in the scene captivated me, the scene itself captured me. It was as if an unseen hand had plucked me from my seat and thrown me through a window where I became suspended — still viewing, still observing, still experiencing, but now immersed in the scene...a part of it.

A shocking transition, to be thrust into a setting that I did not create with my imagination. At first, it was overwhelming. I tried to control things but soon realized I could not. I tried to reach and to grasp — I failed. I tried to walk, to run, to speak — nothing happened. Paralysis overcame me. I became nothing more than a consciousness floating in space while the world went on around me.

I wanted to turn and look around, but I was frozen. My eyes focused on things without my permission. I could see a desk, but not my desk. A man sat at the desk. A fuzzy image, but this man looked familiar to me. I involuntarily turned from the man to face a room full of people sitting at desks. These people too were out of focus, but it was clear that they were looking at me.

Thankfully, but not of my own accord, I turned away from these blurry figures and their staring problems. I turned until my back was to them. From this position, all I could see was a whiteboard.

An invisible force guided my hand to pick up the blue dry-erase marker from the tray below. I removed the cap and began to write on the board, against my will.

I had lost my sense of time. I do not know how long I stood there writing on the board. It could have been minutes or hours, for all I knew. And what was I writing, anyway?

Letters. Numbers. Dots and dashes. Strange symbols, like hieroglyphs.

It reminded me of a mathematical formula. Algebra? Trigonometry? Calculus? I was not sure, but I knew I did not like it. Yet there I was, scrawling out a lengthy calculation across the whiteboard.

I got to the end of the calculation. $x=3.14159265359$.

The invisible force acted on me, and I turned to face the people again. They erupted in laughter. They laughed and laughed. I cannot say how long I was stuck there facing those people and listening to their laughter, their sneers and jeers, pieces of which I could understand.

"It's not x, it's pi," they sneered.

"He'll have x equaling mc-squared before he's done!" they jeered.

I wished for the siren to sound and for all of this to melt away.

Then, in another shocking transition, a vacuum suction broke my suspended animation and pulled me back through the window. The scene began to speed up without me in it. I watched as the footage sped past, faster and faster, until objects were indistinguishable, just blurs of color moving across the screen. Sounds became muddled and turned to static. Then, suddenly, the blinds slammed shut. The sound was muted. Darkness fell and extinguished the light.

I fell too. I found myself laying on the dark floor of The Mind *once again. To my relief, the desk people were gone along with their sneers and jeers. The whiteboard was gone. The formula... it still hung in the darkness, barely visible, like pencil markings on black paper, haunting me.*

THE FOUR Ms

"A weak foundation destroys the work." ~Latin proverb

If you stopped reading here and went out to build success in business, you would probably do okay for a while. The four legs of your stool would support you, initially. Using your confidence, control, creativity, and computers, you might be able to open a discount ice cream truck or an out-of-the-way hot dog stand. Either one of those may be bustling in the summertime, but they won't sustain you through the year, year after year. There must be more to this stool.

Way back in the introduction to this book, we discussed the fact that the stool needs more support to carry the weight of sustained success over the long haul. That is when I introduced you to the Four Ms. If the title of this section didn't remind you of that, I'll remind you again.

To add support to the stool, we will build in some cross-members, which I've previously called *rungs*. The rungs will connect the legs of the stool to one another and lock them in place. I did the math and determined we will need four rungs — the four Ms — to properly support success beyond summer treats or processed meats. Now it's time to get into the details of these four Ms and tighten up that stool for sustained success in business.

Speaking of math

Math is something you should learn if you haven't already. I know it well, and it has helped me a couple of times in my life. Unfortunately for you, I hate it and I will not teach it to you.

Math has helped me tremendously inside of The Mind, but it has failed me miserably on occasion in The World. That is why I won't teach it to you, even though I could. There are people trained in teaching the subject. You can hire one of them or you can pick up a math book and start reading.

No, see? That's the thing about math — you can't just pick up a book and start learning it at your age. There are fundamentals and basic principles you need to know first. These basic principles must be learned before a person learns what math is. Being aware that one is learning math will take the "fun" out of "fundamental," making it mostly mental.

The International Department of Knowledge (IDK) mandates that all humans learn the basics of mathematics by the age of two. Humans who reach the age of two without meeting the minimum requirements for math skills will be placed in foster care and their parents will be arrested. A heavy-handed policy, but one that I fully support.

Math sucks but it is important, and it sucks that it is important

Since I hate math so very much, and since math is necessary for a functioning society, I believe it is better to have toddlers who can count than it is to have adults who can't. With a few exceptions, it is generally true that if you let a human develop the ability to make logical decisions, they will never choose to learn math, and that means we need to start early.

If it were possible to un-invent math, I would have done it a long time ago. It can't be un-invented, because sports, and gambling, and gambling on sports would be boring. So, we're stuck with it.

At least that kind of math has a purpose, a place in the world. If we could leave it at that, maybe I wouldn't hate it so much. People can't just leave it though. They continuously try to use math as an excuse for why physics works.

Here is one example of something that makes me hate math:

$$v_{average} = \frac{\int_a^b v(t)dt}{b-a}$$

That is the dumbest thing I have ever seen in my entire life. Math? I would believe you if you told me this is the musical score to a Beethoven symphony. I have a suspicion Pythagoras is behind this, and I curse his name forever. If indeed this is legitimate math, it is not something that is useful to you as a successful businessperson.

Try this one....

$$\$8 + \$1 = \$9$$

You have a dollar and I have eight dollars. I take your dollar. I now have nine dollars. This is useful on the playground when I steal your dollar and I want to know how many dollars I have. For you, the formula goes like this:

$$\$1 - \$1 = \$0$$

It's useful to you, as well. In fact, it is of utmost importance that you are able to do this kind of math. Can you imagine the embarrassment of thinking you have a dollar, but you don't? Not only would it be a major blow to your confidence, but you wouldn't walk away from the ice cream truck with that popsicle you thought you could afford.

Those last two equations are simple, practical examples of useful math. It's situations like these that make math an important and necessary component of the stool of success. It would be difficult to fathom any readers of this book who couldn't perform these calculations. Most of you can probably solve these equations in your head, without scratch paper. You may have to count on your fingers, but there is nothing wrong with that.

I should warn you, there is inherent danger in doing math in your head. You probably haven't been told this before, but once you read it, it will make sense.

When you perform mathematical calculations in your head, you put Merle, your Imaginary Success Guru, in harm's way. You start pulling numbers from different places and flinging them around your brain, matching them up, organizing them, tossing them around. Multiplying and dividing, remembering to "carry the one." It's like shooting rubber bullets in a round room. Merle could get caught by the ricochet at any moment...and that's just simple math. The more complicated computations you attempt in your head will seem, to Merle, more like being trapped in an outhouse with a flock of angry wasps. The numbers buzz around violently. The products and quotients sting relentlessly.

Do yourself and Merle a favor, get some scratch paper. Maybe try an abacus, although that alone requires a six-week training course. What about a calculator? Use one of those instead of filling the outhouse with wasps by doing math in your head.

Check it out. A calculator is a computer. I think I just swerved into another way we can use computers for good. We can have them do all our math for us. That's a good idea. It solves multiple problems. (See what I did there?)

We can use computers to keep track of scores in sports. Can you imagine if we had to do that in our heads? Well, soccer shouldn't be a problem. If and when a team scores in soccer, and if we are awake long enough to notice, we can probably do that math mentally— one point. But football?

Listen, I know the majority of the globe calls soccer "football." I'm guessing whoever named American football didn't even know the other football existed because the two sports are so vastly different from each other. They have almost nothing in common. It isn't like American football is a variation of soccer. So, some guy invented American football, then discovered the existence of another sport called football, so he changed the name of the original sport instead of thinking of a different name for his. That's such an American thing to do (although the idea of renaming existing things could have been imported from Spain by Frank Garbanzo).

Anyway, keeping track of the scores in football is way harder than keeping track of soccer scores. If you try to track football scores in your head, you will most certainly release the wasps. Touchdown: add six. Extra point: self-explanatory — add one, an extra one. Two-point conversion: add two, but not an extra one, and neither one of those two are extras. A field goal is three points. So how many total points do we have?

Ahhh! Tricked you. Did you try to calculate it in your head? If you listen closely, I'm sure you will hear a muffled buzzing sound in your imagination.

Another thing you wouldn't want to calculate in your head is the payout for your gambling bets. Before you can calculate the payout, you need to know the odds. Before you can know the odds, the odds need to be calculated. I think it is obvious that this entire exercise should be left to a computer.

Let me just point out how computers have interrupted our discussion about math. They continue to try to be involved in everything. In the case of math, I say we let them. They can have math. But I am going to control the discussion and bring it back to the topic of success and math's place in it.

From what I can tell, not all successful people are great at math, but they all use math to some degree. The more important observation I've made is that *all* people who are great at math are successful. So, I guess math is important to success, even though it pains me to admit it. I despise it, but it is necessary. That's why it's one of the rungs that supplement and support the four legs of the stool of success in business.

I am not going to continue explaining math to you. I am not here to do math with you. I am not here to talk any more about math until and unless it is absolutely necessary. But you can bet a flock of wasps it will be necessary at some point.

Do you like M's?

Here is another word that just so happens to start with M, and also happens to play a supporting role in success:

Motivation

Motivation is such a silly concept because it's so stupid.

I say it's stupid because it's just silly. A lot of books are written about motivation, but it really doesn't deserve even one whole book. I bet you've heard of people who speak about motivation. Well, they speak to make it, or give it, or whatever they do. It's so silly and simple and stupid that a paragraph or two ought to suffice. There certainly isn't any earthly reason to go around making speeches about it.

Motivation is the reason we do most everything we do. If we don't have motivation, we dead; we very dead. So therefore, however and whatnot, we all have some motivation for something sometime. Again, if we didn't, we would be killed by our own death.

Thereby heretofore thus-and-such, not wanting to die is the reason, the motivation behind our doing things like breathing, eating, and staying out from under pianos that dangle precariously from ropes six stories in the air. Remaining alive is the sole motivation behind almost all safety precautions that we take. So, you see? Silly. Stupid. You don't need Tony Robbins to motivate you in a 400-plus-page book or a three-hour seminar. You just need to want something to happen or to not happen.

Need to want? Yes, that's right. If you don't want something, you won't be motivated to get it. That doesn't mean you won't get it. You can get diarrhea without any motivation for it. If you get success in this way, then it's just luck, and we will discuss that later.

You need motivation if you ever hope to succeed at success. Hope is not motivation. Wishing for success is not a strategy to obtain it. There is more to it than just the want. You must do something — and you will, if and only if you really want to succeed. What I am saying here is that you have to want it strongly enough that you have no choice but to go after it. If your desire burns hot enough, it will force you into action.

Motivation is that thing between desire and attainment. Oh, you didn't know there was a thing in between there? Well, there is. As I already said, it's motivation. If you desire success, motivation will be the thing that gets you off the couch to attain success. See how it's right in between there? And see how stupid it is to even talk about it? But it is important.

This brings me to the motivation vs. inspiration debate. Not that the two of them are battling each other, it's just that the two words get mixed up, interchanged, misused. The two share a relationship. Allow me to explain.

You can't learn motivation. You can't be given motivation. It's a reflex, a reaction to burning desire. Likewise, you can't learn or be given burning desire, but there is one thing you can be given that might lead to desire and subsequently to motivation. That thing is called inspiration.

It is possible that some people confuse the word motivation with the word inspiration. There are people who earn their living making speeches to motivate others. I've mentioned some of their names, but there are thousands of these people. They are known as "motivational speakers."

I'm sure you are familiar with motivational speakers, and you accept the term without thinking about it. I'm asking you to think about it now. Are these speakers really motivational? If a person can say something to you that causes you to take action in order to achieve something that you want, did they really motivate you? Or did they inspire you?

Calling these people motivational speakers puts them in between your desire for something and the attainment of that thing. I will argue about this until you concede: that is not where these speakers should be placed.

Again, if – and it's a big if – *if* someone can say something to you that causes you to take action to achieve something you want, they must have made you want it more than you did before. Maybe they made the object of your desire seem more attainable by explaining how you have the power to achieve it. They might pump you up, boost your confidence, or use other psychological tricks to make you believe you can achieve that which you desire.

Before the speaker ever speaks a word, you already know that getting what you want will take effort on your part. You know there are obstacles to overcome. If you are not putting forth that effort, if you aren't doing the work to achieve your desire, then you don't want it badly enough. Your desire isn't burning hot enough to drive you to action. You don't believe the thing you desire is worth the effort. Isn't that the root of the problem?

So, the so-called motivational speaker fiddles around with your perception of the obstacles and the extent of the work needed to overcome them. Their words do not change the obstacles or the work, only your perception changes. Because your perception is being manipulated, it will appear as though the obstacles between desire and attainment are shrinking and it will take less work to overcome them. These speakers use sleight of mind, like magicians use sleight of hand, to distract you from what is really happening.

While you are busy marveling at the shrinking obstacles and the reduced workload, you won't notice that your desire to achieve is growing. You are actually being inspired to do the work and to tackle the obstacles that previously prevented you from achieving your desire.

I don't know why these people need to be so underhanded and slippery about it. Why can't they embrace the fact that they are inspirational speakers, not motivational speakers? Why do they have to conceal the fact that they are fanning the flames of desire, not clearing the path to attainment? I think we would all be plenty accepting of speeches that make our desires strong enough to motivate ourselves.

Inspiration can not only boost existing desire, but it can also spark brand new desire. This concept is best illustrated in advertising and marketing. Ever see an advertisement for a taco restaurant and suddenly desire tacos? If you desire the tacos enough, you'll go get the tacos. The advertiser's hope is that you will get their tacos. Maybe you will, or maybe you'll get tacos from a different restaurant. Either way, the tacos you have are a result of inspiration.

In this example, desire is created by the advertisement. That's the inspiration. From there, the desire takes over. If the desire is strong enough, motivation kicks in and takes you to the taco joint to exchange money for the tacos. The tacos, once the desire, are now the achievement. It's a beautiful process, and one that can be applied to achievement of success in business.

Too often we think of inspiration as something that is related to creativity. Don't misunderstand; inspiration is often related to creativity, but not always. Sure, artists are inspired to create their art, we've covered this. But businesspeople can use inspiration to achieve business milestones and build success. They use inspiration as a tool. They can use it to sell tacos, or whatever.

It is important to remember that motivation is something that naturally occurs when desire is strong enough. You can't motivate people. There is no use discussing motivation any further. It would be ridiculous to call a taco commercial "motivational," but it is perfectly acceptable to proudly proclaim how you were inspired to buy tacos.

Inspiration is something you can get and give. It's useful and necessary to support success. It happens before motivation. Here's the whole process:

INSPIRATION → DESIRE → MOTIVATION → ACTION → SUCCESS

I call this the *success generator*. You can see where motivation fits. It's right there in the middle, where I said it would be. It's silly, but it is important. Without motivation, no success.

But look at inspiration. It starts the whole process. In that way, inspiration is more important than motivation. You might find that silly too. You may not even believe inspiration is necessary.

You desire success in business, right? That's why you are reading this. You have the desire. It motivated you to read this book. You're taking action by reading this book. The attainment hasn't happened yet, but the action isn't over. You're going to need to sustain the action for as long as it takes. That means you'll need more and more motivation. Which means you'll need a heaping helping of desire. Inspiration is the thing that will serve up the desire.

That doesn't explain how the desire got there in the first place. Can you even remember what made you want success in business? Maybe not. Maybe it seems as if the desire for success has just always been there. But I bet if you dig deep in your memory banks, you'll find inspiration was behind it all along.

Did you meet someone who is successful in business and respect them? or idolize them? or envy them? Did you realize that gathering shopping carts at the big-box store really sucks and so you decided to find a better living for yourself? Did someone somewhere in your past tell you that you would never amount to anything, so you made it your mission to prove them wrong?

These are all forms of inspiration that might have sparked that first flicker of desire for success in business. We usually think of inspiration as some profound experience, a moment of clarity, hopes and dreams, fluffy words. But inspiration can be simple. It can be almost invisible, or it can be ugly.

Think about it again. What was your inspiration? What made you want success enough to pick up this book? Maybe you are hoping this book will inspire you further, and maybe it will.

First, a warning: If inspiration can be given to you, it may not be given freely. There may be a cost to you in the end, or perhaps the giver will be the one who gains from your inspiration.

Let's look at the taco advertisement example again. The ad provided the inspiration that sparked the desire to have tacos. The desire was yours, the motivation was yours, and so was the action. But the success? Sure, you got the tacos, which is a success for you in that it satisfied your desire. But don't forget, the cost of the tacos was also yours. You gave your money to the restaurant in order to get the tacos. The restaurant also attained success.

Inspired by the profit (not the prophet), the restaurant desired that you buy tacos. In reality, the business desired profit, and it should. Businesses don't make much sense (or cents) without profit. Of course, someone will argue that there are not-for-profit businesses. Like I said, they don't make much sense.

The taco restaurant gave you inspiration through their ad, which created your desire for tacos and motivated you to go to the restaurant and pay for the tacos. That's fine. Tacos probably won't hurt you in moderation. They most likely won't be a detriment to your success. But the example shows the power of inspiration. More specifically, it shows the power of giving inspiration. Inspiring people to desire something that benefits you is like creating a machine that automatically pursues your success for you.

Once the inspiration was set in you, you pursued the desire of the taco restaurant willingly and all on your own. Again, not a big deal. But imagine if someone inspired you to give up your time.

Not-for-profit businesses do this. They inspire people to want to help others for "a cause." They suggest ways to help by "getting involved." This is really just a request for a donation of your time. Except, the not-for-profit business knows that inspiration is much harder to decline than a request. So, they inspire people to want to help and that want becomes motivation to take action. The action becomes eight hours of picking up trash along a highway. That time goes directly to the success of the not-for-profit business. I'm not sure how a clean highway equals success, but we are talking about a not-for-profit business here, so I don't expect logic to play into it.

The point is this; the time you gave to someone else's desire for a clean highway could have been spent pursuing your own desire for success. You let someone else inspire you to a different desire. See how powerful inspiration can be?

Keep your eyes open for inspiration that puts you in someone else's success generator, but also open your eyes to the possibilities. How can you inspire others to get them generating success for you? Therein lies the true power of inspiration. It's just a shame inspiration doesn't start with M.

Momentum

A couple of things about momentum:

- If you look closely, you will see that momentum starts with an M.
- Momentum can only happen after motivation happens.

The first point is barely relevant, but the second thing is important. Motivation drives action. Action gets the ball rolling. Once the ball is rolling, momentum makes it easier to keep rolling. It's like that rule some old guy with a lot of time on his hands made up: "An object in motion will stay in motion unless acted on by another force."

You need to get some momentum, some movement toward your goal, and you need to keep outside forces from wrecking it for you. I have no idea how you will ever do that, but you need to work it out somehow. This is not a joke. Get started and keep on staying started. If anything gets in your way, do something about it. Pretending it isn't there is a possible strategy. If you want success, though, you will need to address any obstacles post haste. You must annihilate the blockstacades to success with the violentational momentumnous force of forward motion. (Not all of these are officially considered to be words.)

You don't need to start out at full speed immediately. Almost no one does that. You start moving towards your goal with one small act. One small forward movement. Then you follow it up with another small act. Then another. Then you take a bigger step, and another. The more forward motion you have the more forward motion you *can* have. That is to say, the more success you get, the more success is available to you.

But, if you aren't prepared for obstacles, they might stop you in your tracks. If you can anticipate and keep up your momentum, you might be able to overcome the obstacles by the sheer force of motion. It's called *velocity*. Having that momentum, that forward motion, and keeping the pressure on to gain speed and force just might give you the power to make it through the barricades. You can easily determine your velocity with this simple formula that I already shared with you:

$$v_{average} = \frac{\int_a^b v(t)\,dt}{b-a}$$

So stupid, and not useful. Sorry, it seemed like I was being too helpful again. That should fix it.

Velocity is just the unit of measure for momentum. Somewhere, out there in The World, there is an ambitious editor who will want to correct me on this. He'll say something like, "This isn't technically true" and he'll spout off with some supporting facts. Relax, David, this isn't a science lesson. Besides, you are correcting the words of an imaginary person.

For the purposes of this book, momentum is forward movement and velocity is the speed of the movement. It doesn't matter, but I wanted you to know what I mean if I occasionally interchange the terms momentum and velocity.

In the success generator, momentum is an important component that drives the process through to the end. It's not just the power it provides to break through obstacles. It also impacts the speed at which success occurs.

Since momentum comes in the action phase of success generation, it typically takes the most time. Inspiration, desire, and motivation can occur in an instant. Action typically doesn't. It starts with one small act followed by another; baby steps. As momentum builds, the steps get bigger. You'll cover more "distance" with each step and the gap between you and success will start to shrink at a faster rate. This is velocity at work. The more you have, the easier it becomes to maintain momentum.

Momentum is inversely proportional to effort.

In the early stages of the action phase, the baby steps are intentional, taking concentration and focus on each little move. After each tiny step, your concentration has to be realigned and you have to refocus on the next tiny step. As you gain momentum, you'll start moving faster and the steps will get bigger. You'll start using less energy with each step. Your concentration will move from the task at hand to the next task while your focus will move from the present to the future. Meanwhile, the present tasks will breeze into the past, completing themselves automatically. Things happen without any further effort on your part. That's when you have the velocity to make a difference.

There are many examples of this concept to be found in everyday life. If you were driving and you wanted to get through a closed gate, would you slow down? Of course not. You would hit the gas and gain as much speed...as much momentum as possible to bust your way through the gate.

Personally, I would stop and try to open the gate unless I really needed to pee or something. You are a violent and reckless lunatic but thank you for providing an example of how momentum works. It's an example of physical momentum versus a physical obstacle. Speed, momentum, velocity, whatever. It's all the same. It is the force that gets the car through the gate and it's the fastest way through the gate.

The type of momentum I'm really talking about here is not physical. When generating success, the obstacles that you may encounter are not always physical either. They aren't imaginary, although I love talking about imaginary things. I'm not sure what to call the state that these things exist in when it comes to the attainment of success in business.

An example of non-physical momentum can be found in the writing of this book. Each time I sit down to write, I start off with just a few words, a sentence. Then I write another sentence. Before long, I have a paragraph and then another. The more words I write, the faster the words come to me. Tens of thousands of words fill the pages before I even know what I'm writing about. It's magical.

Then, an obstacle. Out of nowhere I stumble upon this concept. Another conundrum: What state of existence holds the type of momentum that I use to write this book? It isn't physical momentum. Is it mental momentum? I could stop and ponder it. I could ask more questions or consult other resources, but I won't. I'm moving along with such velocity that I just keep writing and suddenly the answer appears on the page. It's *metaphysical momentum.*

Problem solved. Obstacle conquered. Momentum intact.

There is only one way to get momentum, and that is to start.

Take action. I hope that is clear enough after having said similar things many times previously. I hope it is sinking in.

I cannot teach you to create momentum, but I can tell you this: You must start with one small simple action, then another, and then another. You must sustain the action. Only then will you be swept up in a tide of momentum.

You need momentum if you plan to eliminate obstacles, physical or metaphysical, with brute force. But there are other ways to deal with obstacles. The brute force method is generally preferred unless the better option is to swerve and go around the obstacle in front of you.

What if you could have simply gone around the gate? Your car would be less damaged, and the gate would still be there for those who try to follow. If you want to keep options like this open, you'll need to read the next section.

Mobility

Well look at that! It starts with an M. Really, that's the main reason I've included it here as one of the rungs strengthening the stool of success. I just thought of an M word and went with it. Luckily, I have some wisdom for you based on the word "mobility."

If you somehow happen to get yourself motivated and you get some momentum, you'll need to know about mobility. I am not talking about getting your emails on your smartphone while day-drinking at Shooterz Pub. It's not your ability to videoconference on your tablet from your uncle's funeral. That kind of mobility is for unsuccessful suckers. It simply ensures that you will be expected to work any and all of the time.

I'm talking about the kind of mobility that allows you to change course quickly, to pick up and move when needed, and to escape when threatened. Let's say you're moving towards your goal and you have some momentum, you've built up some steam and you're cruising right along. But then a tree falls in your way. What do you do? Do you have the momentum to plow through the tree? Or should you go around it? Are you mobile enough to leap the tree?

You'll never know if you are moving fast enough to plow through the tree, because it would require the use of the useless formula I've shared twice now. I'm sure you can imagine the results you would get from using something useless. So, if you're going to try to plow through, I guess you will just have to "send it" and find out.

If you think about it, leaping the tree is the same kind of gamble. Are you strong enough to pull it off? You won't know until you either fail or succeed. Which of those outcomes are you hoping for?

Of course, you hope to succeed. And, of course, you know because I already told you, hope is not a strategy for success. For this reason, you need mobility. You need to practice it so you can be confident in your ability to make a split-second decision, to choose a direction without impacting your momentum.

A downhill slalom skier is a physical example of mobility. The skier is blasting down the hill, turning right. Then, in a blink, she is blasting down the hill, turning left. She changes course nearly 180 degrees in an instant without altering the amount of blasting she is doing. In the same way, once you have momentum and you are blasting towards success, mobility will allow you to pivot and reroute yourself when faced with obstacles or when you see a new and better path forward.

Having this type of mobility takes constant effort on your part. Are you sure you wouldn't rather take the easy way out?

If you are cruising along and that tree falls in your path, why not just turn around and go back the way you came? Pick a different route to a completely new location that assures you will not run into that lousy, knocked over, roadblocking tree again. That's way easier, but if you insist on doing it the hard way, I'll show you how.

Practicing mobility

How do you practice mobility like this? You head to the slopes. Get to the mountains, rent some skis and gear, buy a lift ticket, jump out of that giant porch swing and start heading downhill. The first thing you will notice is how easily you will gain momentum. Then, you'll notice how easily your bones break. Witnesses will notice how far and wide your rented gear can scatter across the hillside. Yard sale!

You would think this advice is metaphorical, but I mean it. Go out and try to ski with no training or preparation. That's how you will learn not to take mobility for granted. You'll be wheeled out of the hospital with a new respect for mobility, and you will have less of it than you went in with.

Don't really do that...I lied. I was indeed being metaphorical and the mobility I'm really talking about is metaphysical. Hopefully you didn't follow my advice as soon as you read it. You're supposed to read the whole book before you go out and try the things you learned. If anyone is just picking up this book again after being wheeled home from the mountains, understand that you are doing it wrong.

In order to practice mobility, look no further than your imagination. Look to your Imaginary Success Guru. Merle is blasting down the slopes of success in your mind. Throw in an obstacle and see how Merle handles it. Watch and learn.

I can't know exactly what you have going on in your imagination, but let's say Merle is negotiating a business deal on a yacht in the Caribbean. Everything appears to be going smoothly. Merle has skillfully led the negotiation and it appears the man across the table is about to accept the terms and seal the deal with a handshake. This is a good place for an obstacle, something to test Merle's mobility and see what can be learned.

Imagine a petite woman in a bikini walking up to the negotiation table. She leans over and whispers something in the man's ear. Suddenly, the man withdraws his hand and stares at Merle. No! Better yet, he retracts his hand, reaches under the table and pulls out a gun, pointing it at Merle.

What just happened? All the metaphysical momentum Merle had built toward negotiating the business deal has just been met with a physical obstacle. A gun in the face.

Oh, wow... interesting. What will Merle do?

I would love to know how this ends, but it's your imagination. You tell me. Does Merle use ninja skills to disarm the man, dispose of him, and sail away with the little bikini woman? Does Merle remain in control and use confidence and creativity to disarm the man and get the negotiation back on track?

If your Merle uses ninja skills and steals a yacht, that's physical mobility. You won't learn much from that. Merle isn't in your imagination to teach you martial arts and grand theft yacht. I sincerely hope Merle somehow finds the words that lead to a way out of the predicament and continues toward success in closing the business deal. That fits most appropriately in the subject matter of this book.

Imagine it. Whatever was going on between Merle and that man led to the point where an agreement had been reached. They were ready to seal the deal with a handshake. Then, the swimsuit showed up with some secret to tell the man. The secret inspired the man to want to kill Merle. The man was motivated to draw his weapon, an action that would most certainly change the tone of the conversation.

I just can't stand not knowing how Merle will get out of this. What could possibly be said to diffuse this situation and still get the deal done? Diffusing the situation seems difficult enough, but to continue the business deal would be a masterful display of mobility. Please, when you are finished with this book, drop me a note and let me know how Merle does it. I hate suspense.

Tune in next time to discover the secret of the mini bikini babe on the boat.

Ha! This momentum thing is amazing, isn't it? You never know where it will take you.

That is why you need mobility. To get back on the tracks when the train has clearly jumped them.

I was blasting right along there, explaining ways to practice mobility, then I got caught up in the thrilling scene on the yacht. It could happen to anyone. Now it's time to get back to it.

Using your imagination truly is the best way to practice mobility; metaphysical mobility, that is. You can run Merle through the mill and note the results. There are bound to be some wild times, as you can see.

The mobility you need for success in business lies within your mind. It's a way of thinking, or not thinking. Yes, it's both. If you are still insisting on getting success the hard way, by doing the hard things, I will explain.

Mobility is partly derived from your mental ability to assess what lies ahead and chart a course that preserves your momentum. It's the ability to make decisions quickly. If you can anticipate obstacles before you encounter them, you will be able to make course corrections and avoid many of them. Then it becomes reactive, reflexive. Mobility becomes instinctual, and it must. If you are not mobile, your metaphysical momentum will cause all your metaphorical gear to scatter across the hillside. Yard sale!

I've been talking a lot about obstacles because they are the things that get in our way and threaten our success. Obstacles aren't the only pieces of shit that threaten your success. Oh, no. There is the inevitable piece of shit we call *change*. Some people consider change to be an obstacle, and for that reason it is an obstacle to them. It should not be an obstacle for you, yet it can threaten your success.

"Doesn't that make change an obstacle, then?" you might ask.

No, it doesn't. *You* make change an obstacle. I'm telling you not to do that, but it is a threat to success, nonetheless.

Change has the most impact during the action stage of the success generator, when momentum is building. Momentum builds best when all other factors remain the same. Everything else being equal, a repeated action gets easier each time. That is what makes momentum possible.

When change occurs, momentum is the first thing impacted. Change will slow momentum unless there is mobility to move with the change. That is why it makes sense to discuss change at this point.

Change is going to happen. There is nothing you can do about it. Everything changes other than the fact that everything changes. You cannot control it, and for that reason, change is not included in the "control of everything else" category.

The weather changes. Sometimes it changes rapidly. It has been known to ruin a parade or two.

Technology changes. We touched on some of those changes when we talked about computers, but all technology changes. Computers, automobiles, trash bags (really just the material they are made of), haircuts. (No, that's not technology, that's style. Style changes too though.)

Times, they are a-changin'.

Things will change and the change will affect the way you manage your success. You will need mobility to adapt to the changes and keep moving forward.

The entire Stool of Success will support you through change, but your mobility is the front-line defense against the threat that change poses. Practice, practice, practice. Continuously reapply the things you've learned here in new ways to keep pace with the changes. The changes won't stop to let you catch up.

Now you know

The cat is out of the bag. You know the rest of what you need to know in order to build that solid foundation within yourself — the stool — the platform that will support the success you will inevitably build.

Hold up! It isn't inevitable. You have plenty more to learn. However, if you stopped learning right here, you would still be a stool's height above the rest of the world. Are you satisfied?

I encourage you not to settle for just being this much better than the rest of the world. If you don't stop here, if you strive for blatant and obvious superiority over the rest, then that's what you will have. And I won't stop teaching you until you have it in your sights.

Math, Motivation, Momentum, and Mobility are all M-words. I've capitalized them here because I've capitalized on them in my success experience.

Let's have one more look at the finished product, The Stool of Success in Business.

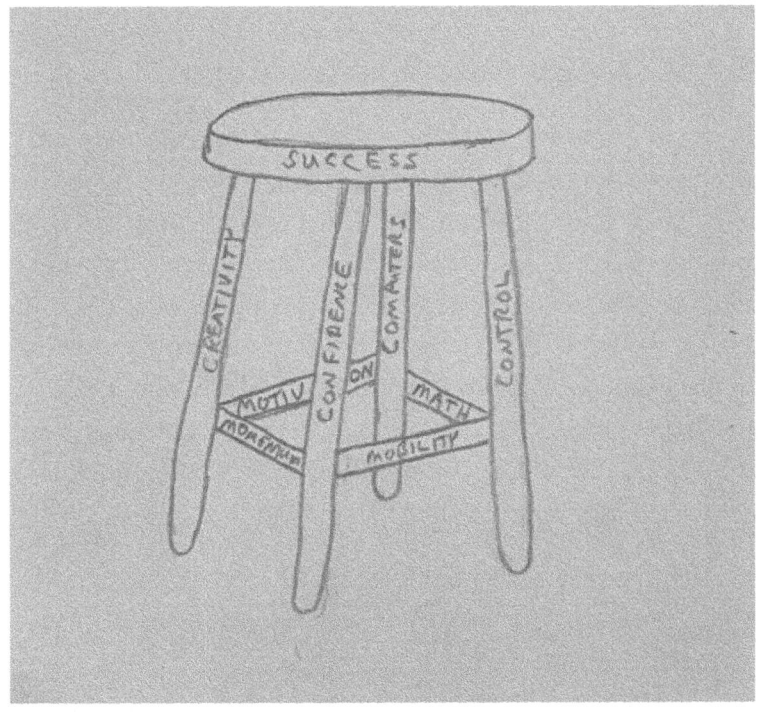

Before I leave this subject, I want to point out something in the illustration. More specifically, I want to point out something that is *not* in the illustration. When you are successful, many people will believe you used this one thing to attain your success and to support it. It's called *luck*.

I could add luck to the illustration. If I did that, it would be a pillow or a cushion on top of the stool. That would appear to make luck a comfy seat…but only if the cushion stays in place. Spoiler alert! It won't stay in place. It will slide around and slip out from under you, because that's what luck does.

The problem with luck

Luck is a tricky little bitch; I'm not even going to lie.

The problem with luck is we can't decide to have it. We can't manipulate it. Some people naturally have the good kind in abundance. Others have the bad kind and seem to spread it all over the place, like leprosy. Some of us have luck sneak up on us once in a while. It might be good luck, it might be bad luck, we don't know until it happens. That sort of unpredictability has no place in a quest for success. You certainly shouldn't rely on good luck to support you. Don't sit your ass on a stool made of luck. You'll probably wind up sitting on the floor, like the Japanese at dinner time. Uncomfortable at best.

So often I hear of mildly and temporarily successful individuals who got their "big break" when something coincidental happened to them.

A musical group may get discovered just because some chubby weirdo producer happened to be drunk in the god-forsaken dive bar where the band was performing one night. They probably had five fans at the time and three of them were the drummer's ex-wives.

Sure, maybe that producer opened a pathway to fame for the band, but now look at them! One guy is in rehab, one guy is dead, the remaining two are going around the country with two other no-name replacements playing the same songs they played 30 years ago.

And what about all that money they made? Gone! Spent it on fun. 30 years of pure, uninterrupted fun. Sounds disgusting. That's no success that I want any part of. Success generated by luck is not success, it's just luck. You'll be lucky if you sustain it for a minute.

I know of people who believe they can manipulate luck. They think finding a penny on the ground brings good luck. They believe breaking a mirror brings bad luck.

Some people conduct certain rituals they believe will promote good luck, like spinning in a complete circle before boarding an airplane. This bogus luck ritual just keeps perpetuating because the planes these people board just keep not crashing. It leads to validation of the belief that the ritual works. In reality, it is the airplane that works. It isn't luck that keeps it in the air.

When you're good, you're lucky

On the flipside, success at my level frequently causes all the jealous haters to believe that I must have gotten lucky at some point to be where I am. Nope. Not one time, ever. Those few of us who have attained this level of success tend to make it look easy. We tend to appear lucky. Things just seem to go our way. What you must understand about this phenomenon is that success breeds success. It snowballs. The more success we have, the more we attract. It has absolutely nothing to do with luck. We are doing this on purpose.

Another minor correction

Wait a minute! I am not completely satisfied with one sentence in the previous paragraph: "It snowballs."

Does it really snowball?

As a general concept, I'd say it does. That's the momentum idea I was talking about. The bigger it gets, the faster it gets bigger. The faster it goes, the faster it goes.

The part of the analogy that bothers me is it gives the appearance that success is rolling downhill. Success is not down, it's up. It's located at the top. It isn't gravity-assisted. No one talks about tumbling down to the valley of success. It's the pinnacle, the summit, the tippy-top. There's not much room up there. That's why you need to push people off when they get close to you.

When I got to the top, there was a guy there. He involuntarily snowballed down to the valley below, and he is not happy about it. Bad luck for him, I guess. King of the Mountain!

Oops. Missed my exit. Where was I headed with this? Oh, yeah! If your plan for success in business involves luck, your plan sucks. You haven't learned anything from what I've been saying here and you're lucky I don't jump out of this page and smack some cents out of you.

Interlude Five

I switched on the light in my imagination, erasing the darkness and with it the ghostly remnants of the mathematical formula to reveal my office just as it was before.

I sat at my exotic wooden desk in my extravagantly comfortable chair, kicked up my feet and stared at the ceiling, replaying the scenes and experiences of the day. Then, for the first time in my existence, I closed my eyes.

The darkness! A "lightbulb" moment!

I opened my eyes again. The ceiling.

Again, I closed my eyes. Again, darkness. I felt a smile form on my face as it hit me... The Mind's eyes!

I thought about the events that I witnessed and had become a part of. Was that The World?

"Yes, it was The World," *answered* The Mind.

"How? Why was I there?"

"I get nervous in front of the class."

I was a little stunned and a lot curious. "You get nervous in front of the class?" I asked. "I don't see how I have anything to do with that."

The Mind was silent for a moment, then responded, "You don't get nervous in front of anybody."

"No, I don't," I said, and then it occurred to me. "Did you bring me along to take your place in front of the class?"

"I did. It didn't help as much as I thought it would."

The disappointment in his voice was obvious.

"Maybe next time you'll let me have some control," I suggested. "I can't help if I'm paralyzed and just along for the ride."

"Fair enough," he said. "Next time I'll let you drive."

"Perfect. Then next time they won't be laughing at us."

I assumed this satisfied him for the time being, since he did not respond. After a minute or two, I spoke again.

"Hey, Mind!"

"Yes?"

"Can you cool it with the sirens?"

"What do you mean?"

Growing more comfortable with the conversation, I said what I meant. "I mean, stop blasting the sirens when I'm trying to work! It's disrespectful."

With a sigh, The Mind replied, "Sorry about that. It's just sometimes you take things too far."

"Says you!" I retorted. "I need space to do what I do."

He paused, then responded. "Just promise you'll be respectful to people."

"Of course I will," I said. "You can trust me."

With that I sat back in my chair and resumed staring at the ceiling. I smiled again. I'll be ready the next time those blinds open.

"That's what I am afraid of..." the voice whispered.

CONCLUSION

Confidence, control, creativity and computers. Math, motivation, momentum, and mobility. These eight things make up the Stool of Success and give it a solid foundation.

Now for the bad news. If you want to be successful, you must master *all* of these — the Cs *and* the Ms. If you've decided that you are willing to do the hard things, then it's time to get started.

Conduct an honest assessment of yourself, right now. Do it! If you find yourself weak in any one of these areas, you will not succeed. Sorry to break it to you, but that's just how it works. You might get away with being slightly deficient in one or two of these if you are super good looking. But you'll need to honestly assess that too. I'm not talking about being somewhat attractive or having an interesting look. I mean *super* good looking... automatically considered gorgeous by 100% of everyone.

This revelation may cause some of you to become discouraged and give up. You know you are lacking in one or more of these areas and you also know that you are not *super* good looking. So, go ahead and give up. It proves for certain that you are lacking in the motivation department. You are also lacking in the departments of confidence, control, and creativity. But you already knew that, didn't you?

A clever, success-seeking person might apply my oft-copied "fake it till you make it" advice and keep going forward towards success despite knowing the truths of your honest assessments.

Some of you did an honest assessment and found shortcomings in many, or maybe all, of these areas, but you refused to admit it. That's precisely the attitude you need. After all, this book has provided you with the tools to turn things around.

I realize some of these areas are harder to master than others. Take **math**, for example. Only a small percentage of people are great at it. An even smaller number of people care about the percentage of people who are great at it and yet — as you learned earlier — math is still necessary.

That means you need to embrace math and be comfortable with it. As I said before, if you didn't learn math fundamentals by age two you should probably hire someone to teach them to you.

If you are inspired enough to want to learn math on your own, get some flash cards or something. Study at home until you can multiply single-digit numbers without using your fingers. Like I suggested, maybe try operating an abacus, it's a lost art. Or is it a science? Either way, can you imagine the surprise on their faces when you pull out your abacus at a party and start mixin' the math right there on the spot? You will impress, and that is a form of success.

Remember, **motivation** is silly and it's stupid to talk about it. If you meet anyone who claims to be a motivational speaker, confront them. Call out those phonies. Ask them why they are hiding their true intention, which is to inspire people.

Inspiration is the beginning of success generation. Get inspired. Fan the flames of your desire for success. That will motivate you.

Once you are motivated, you will act. You'll start with baby steps (like learning math). One small action, then another and another. You will need a healthy amount of self-control at first until you start building **momentum**. You will be moving towards success, and you'll start moving faster and faster. Your steps will get bigger and easier. Don't forget to anticipate obstacles. The faster you are moving, the harder an obstacle will wreck you.

That's where your **mobility** comes into play. You won't know for certain if you are mobile enough until you encounter an obstacle at a high rate of speed. The only way to test mobility for real is to send it and see what happens. If you think about failure at that moment, failure will be the result. Just believe in yourself and go for it, unless you are lazy, in which case you could just turn around and go somewhere else to avoid obstacles.

Confidence comes first. You can't do any of this without confidence. You don't need knowledge, or proficiency, or experience. Be confident, even if you have to fake it, right out of the gate.

Use the process I presented for you to simulate confidence. You'll need to fake it at first, but no one will know you are faking.

Once you've developed the habit of acting confident, start building real confidence. The processes of Confidence Deflation and Confidence Absorption will help you steal confidence from others and make it your own. Get some confidence donors to give you "votes" of confidence. Give yourself confidence using affirmations. Each of these methods build real confidence.

Finally, live confidently. Never doubt yourself. If you find your confidence slipping, call on Merle to help. Always dress like you are already successful. Stand upright, walk tall, let your chest lead. Be proud of yourself and be loud about it.

Control yourself. At any time, you can go back and review the segments of self-control. In fact, until you have self-control mastered you should have the discipline to review those segments on a regular basis, because self-control is necessary to control other people.

Control of other people is remarkably simple if you have confidence and self-control. To control everything else, you need to figure out when to try to control any one particular thing. You need to know if the thing can't be controlled. When something can't be controlled, instead of trying to control it and failing, simply strive to control it forever. That way you won't fail even though you won't succeed.

Everyone has some **creativity** in them. I gave you a couple of ways to test and exercise your creativity. Use them. Use them every day, if you must, until creativity comes naturally. Then, use your creativity to innovate, because with innovation, even failure is success. Get ideas, good or bad, and act upon them. Use the idea machine.

All of you, no matter how old you are, need **computers** if you wish to be successful in business.

The older you are, the more difficult computers will be for you. If you are medium-aged, you probably have some skill by default. The "youngins" already have it figured out, but they don't know it.

One more generation from now, computers will be built into human bodies from birth, so this leg of the stool will go away. I'm sure something will come along to replace it. If not, stools can have three legs, and I will have to update my sketch again.

For the current and existing generations, it's all about word processing and the many facets of the Internet to be used for communication (and sometimes research). These things must be employed to spread your confidence, control, and creativity around the world as quickly as possible and as often as needed.

Avoid spreadsheets! That requires a good amount of self-control, to be sure. But not as much as you will need for the psychological battle to break the will of your computer's artificial intelligence. Once you win that battle, you'll have made friends with the computer. You'll have that leg of the stool installed and ready to support your future success.

It doesn't matter which department you find problematic, the advice I am providing is solution-o-matic. Most of the solutions for your problems have already been provided. Maybe you missed it. You are welcome to go back and read it again. For easy reference, here are few of the key principles that I, Dr. Guff Meister, I.S.G., have provided in this book:

Key principles for building The Stool of Success.

You don't need to be liked. It doesn't hurt if people like you, but what you are really after is respect. Respect is something you command. Either way, your confidence is what will get you the respect you deserve.

Let Merle be Merle. The imaginary person living in your mind will provide you with the guidance and coaching you need to become successful, but you must let Merle do what Merle does. Don't interrupt or stifle any activities Merle is involved in. Let yourself daydream. That's Merle working Merle's magic. Let Merle take over when you find yourself in situations where your stool seems unstable. Trust Merle.

Fake it till you make it. Others have given this advice before me. This time it isn't horseshit. Learn to act confident as a first step towards becoming confident, or just keep acting confident the whole time. No one will know. And this advice isn't limited to confidence. You can fake anything else you need to fake, as well.

If you want someone to do something, tell them to do it. This is about controlling other people. It is the simplest of all these principles and it pays big dividends. Success comes much easier when people do what you need them to do, so just tell them to do it. Tell them confidently in the most intimidating voice you can muster.

Remember these principles when building your Stool of Success in Business. They make the job easier. It still won't be easy. It will take hard work and dedication to attain success, but I've provided the framework to build a platform for that success once you've done the work. Just know that the platform is not the success, it is simply the foundation. You still have work to do to build the success.

Can you believe we are almost to the end of this book, and we haven't even *defined* success? You know you want success in business, but what is that? What does it mean? What is the definition of success?

Well, you can look it up on the Internet and find out that someone thinks it is "the accomplishment of an aim or purpose."

Yes, I suppose that's right, but where does that leave us?

It leaves us with more questions: What is our aim? What is our purpose? We must have these answers before we can know that we have accomplished them.

If your aim is to sell a widget, does accomplishing the sale of the widget constitute success?

Well, sure it does. But it doesn't make the seller successful in business. The seller was successful at selling that one widget. It doesn't mean he will continue to sell widgets over and over again until he reaches the pinnacle of success. Besides, if there is a pinnacle to reach, it would be something set arbitrarily by someone else. The boss man sets the goal and the salesperson aims to accomplish it. Once he reaches the goal, he is successful. Right?

If that's your definition of success, then fine. Hopefully this book will help you. But I am disappointed in you. It isn't your fault. I set standards for you that you couldn't live up to. That's my fault.

Shame on me.

I know there are people reading this who have greater expectations for success in business than just winning sales awards. Some may wish to run a corporation, be the boss. Maybe that is success. Maybe some want to make a certain amount of money or retire comfortably at a certain age. Maybe that is their idea of success in business. It is still disappointing to me.

True Success

The success that I had in mind while writing this book — the success I was expecting readers to desire — is the kind that can *never* be attained.

Hear me out. Don't quit on me now. I know I've been using the word "attain" and speaking of success as a destination, a summit to reach, a goal to accomplish. Those are just terms. There isn't a good way to explain the process of building a platform for success in business without speaking of success in these terms. If I started off from the beginning saying you will never attain the level of success I'm speaking of, would you have continued reading the book?

I'm talking about a type of success that is perpetually on the horizon — a destination that moves away each time you come close. To be clear, the success doesn't move itself. You move it.

Each time you think you've reached your goal, set a new one. Desire success, get motivated to get it, take action, attain the goal. Then, realize you aren't finished. Realize you desire more and do it all over again.

If your goal is to sell a widget and you do that, don't stop there. Set another goal further away. Sell *all* the widgets. Then move the goal even further. Become the leader of widget sellers in the company, the ever-coveted "sales management" position. Once you do that, set the definition of success to owning the company. Once you own the company, set your sights on taking over a competing company, acquiring a supplementary company, growing the conglomerate to a certain revenue level.

See how that type of success grows and builds. It keeps you constantly moving towards it. As you keep chasing it, you will not become complacent or content. You will not rest on your laurels or settle for what you've accomplished. You will keep going. And when you tire, when you run out of gas, you'll look back and see a mountain of success. A beautiful, heaping pile of success that cannot be denied by anyone.

What good does that do? You're tired and you're out of gas. Will you even get to enjoy the fruits of your labor?

There are people who want it this way. To them, it's the journey, not the destination. They take pride in stringing together hundreds of individual successes. It's the thrill of the chase.

Even when they are worn out and no longer able to chase after the next success, they don't stop. They start looking at their legacy. They find ways for their success to continue to grow, to become bigger than themselves. They set up systems and processes and put people in place to continue hitting milestones and aiming at the moving target of success.

To some, true success is found in leaving their heirs with a head start. They believe the momentum they create can be passed down to their children so the children can continue to chase success at the same and increasing velocity. It doesn't always work out that way, but it is a noble goal. I am not sure how anyone would do this with children, or why. Maybe it's the free labor. Very costly free labor.

I really want you to have the type of success that will outlive you. But something needs to be done about the tiredness and out-of-gasness that results from the pursuit.

Here's one possible solution: Start setting up those systems and processes and put those people in place to start building your legacy now. Right now! You have the foundation to start building it. The specifics of how to do that are for another book. But, if you can build to a level of success that takes on a life of its own, one that keeps building without you, you can afford to stop and enjoy the mountain of success behind you, and the one in front of you. You can enjoy the view from the pinnacle, one of many pinnacles to come.

That is the concept for my definition of success. It's a sustained string of accomplishments that self-perpetuates without further effort from me. Once the success generator is primed for a legacy of success, it should chug along on its own.

Getting to that point might be a long, bumpy road, but if you get lost or stuck, you have the S.O.S - the Stool of Success.

Okay, this road metaphor just won't die. It's resilient. Just like you, now that you've reached the end of the book.

I'm glad you stuck with it, and I hope it sticks with you.

Good luck!

Just kidding.

The End

Epilogue

I landed gracefully on the floor of The Mind *after being vacuumed out of another exciting visit to* The World.

On this trip I had single-handedly convinced the House of Representatives to propose legislation making it illegal for anyone to put pineapple on pizza, and I was feeling quite satisfied with my accomplishment.

I wasted no time lying there in the dark.

I quickly manifested a swimming pool on the rooftop of the 47-story Crock, Inc. Headquarters building, where I would celebrate my accomplishment.

I arranged lounge chairs, tables with umbrellas, and various other outdoor furniture around the pool and added pergola structures in strategic places, providing some shady areas to rest and enjoy the scenery.

I imagined tropical plants gently swaying in the breeze around the perimeter of the pool area, and the tropical plants appeared.

A two-tier cabana bar sat to the north end of the pool. The lower tier featured a swim-up bar while the upper tier was of the open-air walk-up variety.

I sat back in a lounger under the pergola nearest the bar and motioned to a beautiful cabana girl wearing a grass skirt...and nothing else. She nodded and shuffled off to the bar, soon returning with a Bourbon Smash cocktail, which she handed to me.

"Can I get you anything else, Doctor?" she asked sweetly.

"No, thank you, my dear. That's all for now."

I sipped the drink, then sat back in the lounger and took a deep breath. The tropical plants danced gracefully, and the cool air moved over me.

"What a fabulous day," I thought to myself. "Another success in The World."

"Yes indeed. Feels great," came the reply from all directions at once. "We're getting good at this."

"We? We're getting good at this?"

I laughed.

"Okay, you are getting good a this," The Mind responded. "But I made you, so I deserve some credit."

"I'll give you that."

I sat quietly for a moment, enjoying the shade and sipping my cocktail. The Mind was quiet as well.

Before long, he broke the silence. "We've been doing this quite a while now, haven't we?"

"If you mean succeeding, then yes, we have." I answered. *"We've been succeeding my whole life."*

After another moment of silence, he spoke again.

"Hey, remember the job interview?"

"The one where I got you your current job? Of course, I remember. I was brilliant that day, standing in for you."

"Yeah. It was awesome," he responded with excited nostalgia. *"Not only did I get the job—"*

"...You got a date with the interviewer," I interrupted.

"Ha-ha! I sure did."

"Not only did you get the job and a date," I said, *"you also got a wife out of the deal. I told you not to do that, but you did it anyway."*

He chuckled again.

"It's all good. Things turned out for the best, I think."

He continued, "How do you do that?"

"Do what?"

"Succeed all the time. It's like you never lose."

I thought about the question for a minute and then answered, "It just comes naturally to me. I'm just built for it."

"Well, you have me to thank for that," he quipped.

"I suppose I do," I replied.

"You know?" He began again. "Something about our partnership just works. Do you think anyone else could do what we do... as far as being successful all the time?"

Again, I thought for a moment, then answered, "I am sure I could teach someone the process."

"Wait! There's a process?"

The Mind *was incredulous.*

"Yes."

"And you can teach it?"

"Yes."

"Oh, damn!" he said, still incredulous. "We should write a book."

He had barely finished the sentence when the tropical plants disappeared. The pergolas and the cabana bar collapsed to nothing. The outdoor furniture faded from view as the pool and its surroundings receded into the black.

All was quiet.

Then, the blinds of The Mind *were thrown open — the darkness shrieked and fled. The light rushed in along with the wind, grabbing me and pulling me out through the window into* The World.

When the dust settled and the wind stopped, I found myself sitting in front of a computer.

A cursor blinked on an otherwise blank screen.

I was compelled to type.

A single sentence appeared — just three words...

"There was darkness."

ADDITIONAL OPPORTUNITIES

What happens if you've taken in all the information and the lessons from this book, but you still want more?

I have anticipated that you may want to enhance your success-building capabilities beyond these lessons, so I have provided some additional opportunities for learning and growth here.

Confidence Double™ Certification

The term "Confidence Double" is a registered trademark of the non-existent Crock, Inc.

A Confidence Double is a formally-trained imaginary person who lives inside the mind of a host but can also stand in for the host when displays of confidence are needed. I've referred to Merle as your Confidence Double many times throughout the confidence section of this book. Hopefully I have explained what this means in an understandable way, and you have created your own Confidence Double.

In order to legally call your imaginary helper a Confidence Double, that imaginary helper needs to be officially certified in confidence-doubling. Crock, Inc. offers an imaginary 12-week training and certification course which your imaginary helper may attend to become certified and legally operate in your mind as an official Confidence Double™.

Your imaginary helper will serve you well as it is, but you won't be able to claim the elite status that comes with a certified Confidence Double. Most successful people love the prestige of having their imaginary helpers certified through this program. The certification course is not meant to improve the way your helper operates, rather it is a status revered in many circles as a "must have" for successful people.

For more information on this certification program please visit crockinc.com.

Imaginary Success Guru™

As you may have noticed while reading the book, I referred to Merle as your confidence double during the confidence section, but after that, I began using the term "Imaginary Success Guru." This is because Merle helps you with more than just confidence.

Merle helps in all facets of the success-building. That is why Crock, Inc. offers an additional certification program to upgrade your duly certified Confidence Double to a duly certified Imaginary Success Guru.

There is no required classroom or online training to obtain this additional certification, but there is a one-time $999 upgrade fee. Again, this is a play for prestige, not a beneficial improvement to Merle.

As a bonus, once certified, your Imaginary Success Guru will be able to include the initials "I.S.G." after his or her name. You can even add "Dr." before their name if you want, just like yours truly. I assure you this is the cheapest way to do that.

To apply for ISG certification your certified Confidence Double must be in good standing and up to date with all continuing educational activities. See crockinc.com for more information.

Confidence Deflation™ and Confidence Absorption™

These terms are also registered trademarks of Crock, Inc. The concepts that these terms represent were presented to you, on a surface level, during the confidence lesson of this book. For deeper understanding, you may wish to attend the Crock, Inc. Confidence Deflation and Absorption master class.

In this master class, you will learn how little you actually know about Confidence Deflation and absorption. You will learn how unworthy you are to attend the class and how you should have paid more attention during the portions of the book where these terms were discussed. Once the class is complete, I will thank you for the confidence you leaked into the room, which I absorbed.

All of this can be yours for a modest, one-time enrolment fee of $5,500, along with a supplies and consumables fee of $6.

The eight-hour classroom session is offered every Tuesday beginning at 8am. For locations and enrollment information please visit crockinc.com.

Abacus Training

This six-week online course will have you mastering the lost skill of sliding magical colored beads this way and that. It will have you doing complex mathematical computations in an inconvenient and labor-intensive way so that it seems impressive to those who witness it.

Upon completion of this course, you will be able to multiply single-digit numbers using the abacus. This will allow you to begin mixin' the math at parties and social functions, which will build real confidence and win many admirers.

If you don't have an abacus, they are available for lease with course registration. As an option, you may contact the abacus sales team (info below) to order an abacus of your very own. These quality abaci come with custom-carrying cases and personalized brass nameplates. Ranging in price from $899 to $14,999, we have the abacus that is right for you.

Financing is available at reasonable interest rates, so you don't have to outlay a bunch of cash right up front.

Crock, Inc.

Abacus Sales Team

+1 (101)-555-2202

Horse-lifting boot camp

Physical fitness is not as important to an imaginary person as it is to a real person, but I understand the desire for those of you in The World to be in shape. That is why I have developed a fitness training program for you, and so that you can back up any outrageous claims made by your Confidence Double.

If you are going to tell people you can lift a horse and half, it would be beneficial to your confidence if you could lift a horse and a half.

Many of you are wondering what circumstances might arise that would make this skill necessary. It will never be necessary other than to back the claim that you can do it, or to win a bet. Still, the concept seems so strange, doesn't it? Maybe lifting a horse makes a little bit of sense, but why a horse and a half? Where would one find half a horse?

Typically, I wouldn't get into to technical aspects of my programs, but I can see there are many questions about this.

The secret to lifting a horse and half is to lift two quarter horses and a whole regular horse. You're right when you say to yourself, "That's three horses."

It is three horses. It's even more impressive than your original claim seemed at the time you made it. If you tell people you can lift a horse and a half and then *show* them that you can lift *three* horses, the amazement that fills them will force out the vast majority of any confidence they might have had, and you will absorb it.

Join my Horse-lifting Boot Camp, offered Mondays at 5:00am in the HQ fitness center. To sign up, write your name on the list taped to the refrigerator in the 12th floor breakroom.

I know it looks like a list of people and the side dishes they will bring to a potluck, but it's the boot camp sign up, I assure you. There was some confusion when the list began...people started naming sides that go well with horse. I'm sure they were thinking the half a horse thing was really half of a horse...like a side of beef...except not beef.

An idea for you

The discussion about mail and email and texts in the "Computers" section of this book inspired an idea.

That section is really about messages, written messages. It's about communication between people.

With both mail and email, the originator of the message sets the destination of the message, the address. They determine where the message goes and who receives it. But think about the message in a bottle.

Somewhere on a desert island far, far away, a stranded stranger scribbles a message on a piece of dried seaweed, using a fish bone as a pen and his own blood as ink. Once the blood dries, he stuffs the seaweed in a dirty old bottle he found on the beach. He seals the bottle and tosses it in the ocean.

Thousands of miles away, years later, a kid finds the bottle on the beach. She opens the bottle, takes out the seaweed, tosses it on the ground, and proceeds to fill the bottle up with sand and water. She gleefully fills the bottle and pours it out, over and over, playing with it.

Message not received! The sender didn't even know who he was sending it to or where. A very inefficient and extremely unreliable method of communication. But apparently it works once in a while, which brings me to my idea.

I am acting upon my idea and doing a little development, but not too much. My intent in acting upon this idea is to simply give it to you. Whoever wants to take this idea and bring it to life in The World, feel free. You can have it.

The idea is to create some kind of digital message-in-a-bottle system. What if I could write a message in an email with a computer and send it on a random, unknown journey through the invisible pipeline and have it "wash up" on a virtual, digital beach somewhere? And then someone somewhere far away could virtually "stumble" upon my message, perhaps years later.

Well, that might be pretty cool. Just an idea. You and Merle can have it, run with it, be successful.

See you at the beach.

What's Next?

Shhhh! It's a secret. There is another book coming!

Just kidding, it's not a secret. Tell everyone. Shout it from the rooftops!

Here are a few things you can do to stay informed and keep the momentum going:

1. Sign up for email communications from me with updates on this and future projects by typing this secret code into the search bar: subscribepage.io/DAn10G

2. Tell friends and family about the book.

3. Leave a review at your book retailer of choice.

4. Follow me on Facebook @ryanguffeyauthor

5. Visit my website at ryanguffey.com[1]

6. Explore the world of Crock, Inc. at crockinc.com and facebook @crockinc

---

1. http://www.ryanguffey.com

Printed in the USA
CPSIA information can be obtained
at www.ICGtesting.com
CBHW032228221023
1445CB00004B/18